'Reynolds astounds in a s

A mighty exaltation to

community that fosters it.'

Publishers Weekly

'**Rich, tender** . . . Neon narrates with clarity, sensitivity and humour. **Warm, heartfelt and fully engaging**.'

Kirkus

'Who wouldn't want a first time partner like Neon? He's tender and sweet and scared and funny. He's romantic. **This is what it could be, should be**, if only we were all as lucky as Aria. Girls (and everyone) wait for your Neon!'

Judy Blume

'With the **authenticity, poignancy, and beauty** often found in his work, *Twenty-Four Seconds From Now* **will stay with readers for years to come**.'

Angie Thomas

PRAISE FOR JASON REYNOLDS

WINNER – YOTO CARNEGIE MEDAL

WINNER – INDIE BOOK AWARD

WINNER – NAACP IMAGE AWARD

5-TIME CORETTA SCOTT KING HONOUREE

'Reynolds is a master at making us feel at home
in other people's neighbourhoods.'
The Times

'Masterful.'
The Washington Post

'Evocative and insightful.'
The Scotsman

'An author to watch.'
School Library Journal

'Gorgeous meditation on the meaning of family, the
power of friendship, and the value of loyalty.'
Booklist

'Moving and thought-provoking.
An author worth watching.'
Kirkus

ALSO BY JASON REYNOLDS

Oxygen Mask

All American Boys (cowritten with Brendan Kiely)

The Boy in the Black Suit

When I Was the Greatest

Long Way Down

Long Way Down: The Graphic Novel

For Every One

Look Both Ways

The Run series:

Ghost

Patina

Sunny

Lu

The Stuntboy books:

Stuntboy, in the Meantime

Stuntboy, In-Between Time

First published in the US by Atheneum, an imprint of
Simon & Schuster Children's Publishing Division in 2024
First published in the UK in 2024
by Faber & Faber Limited
The Bindery, 51 Hatton Garden
London, EC1N 8HN
faber.co.uk

Published by arrangement with Pippin Properties, Inc.
through Rights People, London

Typeset in Garamond Premier
Printed in the UK by CPI Group (UK) Ltd, Croydon, CR0 4YY

A CIP record for this book is available from the British Library

ISBN 978-0-571-39068-7

Printed and bound in the UK on FSC® certified paper in line with our continuing commitment to ethical business practices, sustainability and the environment.
For further information see faber.co.uk/environmental-policy

2 4 6 8 10 9 7 5 3

TWENTY-FOUR SECONDS FROM NOW

JASON REYNOLDS

faber

For my friends.
And our firsts.
And Judy.

A lover tries to stand in well with the pet dog of the house.

– Molière

Right now

I swear. If there was a category in the yearbook for *Ugliest Dog Ever*, you would have no competition. None. It'd be you all day. Because you . . . *ugly*. I mean, them eyes alone are enough to win the superlative. All wonky and whatnot. They somewhere between half sleep and fake mean. Somewhere between madness and . . . *madness*. Glaring at me like we got some kind of problem or something. But let me be clear, your crooked look don't scare me. Neither do them cement chips you got for teeth. Look at you. *Most Likely to Scare . . . Nobody*. Or at least not me. What I look like being worried about some stringy-haired mutt with an underbite severe enough to double as a bottle opener? Or Halloween fangs? Or whatever else is supposed to give off scary but ain't scary at all?

At least not to me. At least not tonight.

Tonight ain't for fear. Or for your face. Tonight is for. For us. Me and Aria. Aria and me. Tonight is for. For the winners of the *superlative* superlative. Which is *Most Likely to Like Each Other the Most.* Love each other. The most. And do. The most. Or more than usual. For each other. With each other. Tonight is for our first time and will be *our* first time. Together. *Together* together. And I'm ready. *Ready* ready. I think. I *think* I'm ready. I am. Ready. Except. For some reason . . . I'm still jammed in this bathroom, having a square-up and a stare-down with you like we enemies in a cowboy flick or a hood classic, which are basically the same except for the colour of the characters and the hats they got on.

You looking at me, head cocked like we got beef over turf. Like you got an issue with me being here even though this isn't even your house no more. Still, I can hear you yapping in my ear, trying your best to mess this up. Blow the mood. And that makes me feel ridiculous, because you ain't even *here* to interrupt me and Aria. You ain't even here to get in the way. You just some picture stuck in the metal frame of the medicine cabinet mirror, curling at the corners. And yet I swear – I *swear* – if there was a category in the yearbook for *Worst Distraction During an Important Moment*, you'd also win that one. Because I'm definitely distracted. Standing here in my underwear, curling at the corners too. At least that's what it feels like. And I wish curling up was the only feeling I'm feeling. But it's not. I'm feeling. Stuff. More than I think I thought I would. More than anybody ever said.

For instance, how come nobody told me my fingers would tingle or that my face would burn? Why nobody said I would feel all the blood in my body? Feel all my veins spark like electrical wires from temple to toe? Like fireworks under my skin? How come nobody said that just before I . . . connected . . . with my girlfriend, she, who I've seen almost every day for the last two years, would look exactly how she looked the day I met her? That all of a sudden, my eyes would reset? Or maybe her face has reset and suddenly she looks better than good? Don't get me wrong, Aria *always* looks good. Or, I always like to joke, gooder than I don't know what. But tonight, for some reason, she looks different. She looks dazzling. That's what I told her, and no lie, when I said it, her face became a diamond. And she sparkled at me, then kissed me and told me I looked dazzling too. And I tried not to laugh or look down because ain't nobody ever said *that* to me before. And even though she said it, I don't feel it. I don't feel dazzling at all. I feel sick. And excited. But mostly sick. But really excited too. Like what it must feel like, in fact, to be a tiny, ugly, distracting dog like you, Denzel Jeremy Washington. Especially when somebody comes to the door, and your whole body turns into a motor. Or maybe this is what it feels like to be an alarm clock just before wake-up. Sixty seconds before it's time to sing. To make noise and rattle the room and welcome the morning. But the anticipation of that ring makes that last minute the length of the entire night.

I feel. Like that. In fact, I hope there ain't no snooze button on this moment. But if there is, if Aria hits it and holds off this rise-and-shine, that's okay too. If she wants to do this at a different time, or just kiss or whatever, or do other stuff. Or whatever. I'm good with whatever she wants, as long as I make it out of this bathroom alive. Because it feels like something's boiling in my belly, trying to take me out. And this ain't the time or place for dying or diarrhea.

Not here. Not now. Not right across the hall from her bedroom.

Nerves got some nerve showing up. Tonight of all nights. I said nerves, not fear. There's a difference that I won't even try to explain to you because you wouldn't understand. Because you a dog. Matter fact, if there was a category for *Least Likely to Understand*, you would win that one too! Actually, maybe you'd tie with Dodie, but still. Plus, I don't owe you no explanation and don't got time to give you one even if I did, because she in there waiting, while here I am, whisper-shouting at you! A *photo* of you.

Here I am gazing into the toilet, just in case those fries I had a half hour ago decide to exit through the chimney and not the basement door.

Here I am running laps from toilet to sink, sink to toilet, a three-step mile that got me all out of breath.

Here I am wondering what she's in her room doing. What she's thinking. If she's wondering where I am. If it feels like there are teeth stuck in her throat. If there's a ceiling fan in her gut. If she's re-ponied her ponytail or checked the chicken on her breath.

Here I am.

Wondering how I got water all over the floor in here.

And if I remembered to put lotion on my legs.

And if I've licked my lips too much and now they smell like spit.

And I have to remember not to rip the condom open with my teeth like in the movies. Only had to practise that once to know it's a bad idea. Don't nobody want a kiss to taste like a tire dipped in Vaseline. That could *actually* kill the mood.

And if I *do* rip the condom open with my teeth like in the movies, I have to remember to be careful not to bite a hole in it.

And I have to remember to put it on right on the first try. She'll be watching. Pinch and roll. No fumbles.

And I have to remember, a bra is the most complicated lock to pick. So don't bother trying.

Which is why, which is why, which is why I should just

go in there and tell her. Just get myself together, dry my hands and face on the back of this towel, walk into her room, and say it. That I, Neon Benton, her boyfriend of two years,

am nervous. As shit. That's me.

The Most Nervous First-Timer.

Shit.

I forgot to put lotion on my legs.

Lucky for me, she loves me. She loves me enough to tell me I look dazzling and mean it. Ashy and all. Part of me wants her to tell me I look good. Just regular good. Put my feet back on the floor. But also tell me I look gooder than she don't know what. That my body's okay for her.

That it's enough.

Shit.

I hope this lasts longer than a song.

Get out your head.

I hope this feels like a song I can't get out my head.

Or a good movie, with a better sequel. And no actors. And a loose script that begins maybe with some kissing in the hallway of her empty house. Or maybe with chicken tenders for her, fries for me. Or maybe with me at the door, knocking, waiting to tell her she looks dazzling, because she does.

Cut to:

Me, in the mirror, imagining what happens next. Talking to a picture of a dog I swear is barking, knowing I have to leave this bathroom. Taking deep breaths. Waiting on my stomach to quiet. Hearing the playlist she just started. Thinking about whether we'll keep the lights on or turn them off. Or maybe have just a little light. Wondering if she'll let me look at her. Before. And if she'll look at me. Before. And if we'll look at each other the same. After.

Just twenty-four seconds ago . . .

I was rushing to the bathroom and shutting the door behind me. And taking a deep breath, then another deep breath, then another. And giving myself a piece of my mind.

But just before all that, I was peeling my lips off Aria. Off her mouth and her neck and her face and her shoulder and her other shoulder and her face and her neck and her mouth. And her forehead. Because I even kissed her there, which wasn't really my smoothest move because don't nobody be kissing foreheads but fathers. I know this because my dad kisses me and my sister on our foreheads whenever he's in his feelings, and I've even seen Aria's dad do the same. So it's clearly a dad thing. But I'd be lying if I said it wasn't also a me thing. It is. And I'd be lying twice if I said Aria's forehead was the first forehead I'd kissed. It wasn't.

I also kiss my grandmother, Gammy, on her forehead every day. It's how I say good morning to her and also goodbye before I leave for school. It's also how I remind her fading mind that we love it and want it to stay as long as possible.

'Ain't that right, Gammy?' I ask, peppering her forehead, *muah* after *muah*.

'That's right!' she says, all smiles.

Aria, on the other hand, ain't no old lady even though she sometimes acts like one – a million pieces of candy in her bag, big hugs, and the look she gets whenever she knows you know better than to do whatever it is you think you about to do. Despite all that, Aria's far from a grandma. But she smiled when I kissed her forehead too. Not some wholesome smile like Gammy's and not a fake I'm-just-trying-to-be-nice smile either. This smile was welcoming. And mischievous. And sexy. Very ungranny-like, that's for sure. It was such a simple gesture, but it made me feel like I'd done the right thing. And I wanted to do the right thing. All the right things.

And just before the forehead kiss, I'd grown a few extra

hands, and explored the back of Aria's neck and the small of her back and her butt but tried not to focus too much on her butt because my sister told me to remember to not be so damn predictable. Even though, unpredictably, Aria grabbed mine. I won't lie, it made me laugh a little because ain't nobody ever grabbed my butt before, and I wasn't sure how I felt about it but ain't feel enough about it to tell her not to do it, and instead minded the business of my own hands, searching for everything. But trying not to find anything. Because to find something, to focus on something for too long, would turn Aria into a body. *Just* a body. Another note from my sister.

'Okay, so what you thinking about now?' Aria asked, her hands still back there, her lips whispering the smell of tender into my nose. She'd already pushed her sweatpants to the floor and stepped out of them like she was breaking free from a heather-gray cocoon. As if she were hiding wings. Next went the T-shirt over her head, the ponytail the last thing loose. My jeans and shirt were already gone, a wrinkled mess down the hallway where all this began.

We pressed against each other, skin on skin except for

the skin separated by three thin pieces of cotton. Mine, the most blah of the bunch, had an exhausted waistband and was way looser than it was supposed to be but growing tighter and tighter by the second. Hers were mismatched, which was so Aria.

We'd been here before. Not exactly like this, and not in Aria's bedroom, which looks more like a hotel room. Or a guest room. Stale. Bland. But not her fault. Or her taste. Aria's about colour. About pattern and playfulness. About homeyness. Fly. But her mother, Mrs Wright, ain't about none of that. She's more . . . drown. Drown in *Be somebody else!* Drown in *You're not focused enough!* Drown in *How come you can't be more like . . . and like . . . and like . . . ?* So Mrs Wright is the tidal wave that makes sure Aria knows that as soon as high school is over, she'll be washed out of this house, and her room will become a space for visitors. Even though there were never any visitors. And probably would never be any visitors. Because her house – well, her *mom* – isn't really the visitor type. Either way, Aria can't wait to be a goner, to leave home and never have to deal with her mother's *never enough-ness* again, which is why she ain't really care that her room had already been prepped for her exit.

It's decorated with a platform bed, low to the ground, with one of those headboards that look more royal than relaxing. There are framed pictures of musical instruments above it. And above the desk. And on the other side of the room is one of those closets that's . . . outside of the closet. A clothing cabinet, which is like a treasure chest of cozy sweats and hoodies, and I'm sure some other things too. And underneath it all, there's an area rug I swear be in every area of every house with a guest room. Blue, burgundy, and gold. Next to it, a plant I used to think was real, but I should've known better because Aria's entire bedroom looks like it's been staged for a photo in one of them furniture magazines. Like something straight out of a showroom.

My bedroom looks like something straight out of a show*down*. It still has all the stuff of a thirteen-year-old – movie posters and action figures – even though I'm a seventeen-year-old, which means absolutely nothing because the only difference between thirteen and seventeen is that thirteen is when the horny starts, and seventeen is when you're lucky enough to do something about it. Maybe. And that fact alone made me occasionally line up the sneakers that were strewn across the floor, or make the bed, or organise the dresser drawers, which acted less like dressers or drawers and more like cubbies to hide the clothes I never folded and the socks that had lost their mates and had now been turned into cotton crackers after cleanup on the nights (and mornings) I'd dreamed of this moment with Aria.

I'd always imagined that this me-and-Aria thing, this connection, would happen at my house, which now seems like the most unromantic thought ever. And the fact that we'd fooled around there so many times feels like a miracle now that I think about it, and like an act of desperation now that I *really* think about it.

Me and Aria wanted each other. No other way to say it. We wanted each other, bad. And we'd made out so much that, after a while, we were over it. Okay, not *over* it, because nobody ever gets *over* making out. But after a while, *out* became the norm. I lived in *out*. We lived in *out*. Been in *out* for the last two years. Eventually, the only thing the two of us could think about whenever we were making out was, how we could make *in*.

Like I said, we'd been here before. Not exactly like this, and not in Aria's house, but in mine. And in my sister's car – funky with vanilla tree – on a backstreet when my mother was asleep. And at our friends' houses, using parties as excuses for rendezvous. And also in the movie theatre – greasy-lipped from fake butter – 'watching' a film where these sorts of scenes play out way different than what's happening right now in Aria's room.

If this were a love scene in the movies, the music would already be playing by now. It would've come out of nowhere, a soft piano and sweeping horn, and me and Aria would've started kissing in rhythm to the song as if it were playing in each of our minds and could be heard through the holes in each of our ears. In the movies, kisses always seem so aggressive. So hungry, like the lovers be trying to eat each other's faces. Always tearing at each other's clothes, and either one person pushes the other onto the bed, or, in full embrace, they fall onto the mattress like a chopped tree into a pile of leaves.

And no one ever stops to get a rubber. No one ever stops.

But this wasn't the movies. This was really happening. There was no music playing yet. Our kisses were careful. Taking off our clothes – at least the first layer – was a simple process without snags or holes. We hadn't quite made it to the bed and instead were standing, hot and cold, in the middle of the room. The soon-to-be guest room. And I felt like one, a visitor, who wanted to make himself at home but was still figuring out which light switch did what.

If this were a movie, there would've been beams of moonlight cutting across our faces. And our bodies would've become shadows dancing on the wall. Perfect silhouettes. Seamless choreography.

But for us, there were no directions, no directors saying how and where to move.

'Tell me what you thinking,' Aria repeated.

'What I'm thinking right now?'

No one to yell, *Action!*

'Right now,' Aria said, eyes on eyes.

No one to yell, *Cut!*

Because this was real life. And in real life, as excited as I was for this moment, I also felt like I might, I might, I might stop . . . breathing. Keel over and go to heaven right before I get to heaven.

'I'm thinking . . . I'll be right back.'

And twenty-four minutes before that . . .

I was standing in front of Aria's house. Just standing there, staring at the weird door knocker, which was in the shape of a whole note. As in the musical symbol that tells you to hold one note for four counts. It always looked more like an eye to me, and even though I knew it wasn't an eye, I still locked in on it as if it might suddenly come to life and look at me like I had no business being there. And as if the eye/whole note ain't strange enough, it's on a hinge so that it can be lifted and banged against the pink wooden door. Because the door is . . . pink. But not just the door, the . . . whole . . . house. Pink. The colour of tongue. Funny thing is, I remember when it was painted lemon yellow. And before that, lime green. And it was something else before that – I think Aria told me it was purple – which is why it's a good thing the door knocker's made of brass and can go with any colour.

Even though it's versatile, the whole note looks a whole mess to me. But it's not on my front door, and it's not really a weird choice for the Wrights, because Aria comes from one of them musical families. The kind you see in talent shows or on the internet, and they either seem cool because they're not your family or corny because they're not *your* family. In Aria's case, it's . . . both. Her mother is a *world*-famous trumpet player (Trumpeteer? Trumpeter? Trumpetist?) – at least, that's what everybody says, even though I never been around the world to ask if anyone outside of America has ever heard Mrs Wright play the horn. But according to my parents, she's *world*-famous, even though I never heard them listen to a single note of trumpet music. Ever. Not a honk. The newspaper says Mrs Wright's *world*-famous too, even though the newspaper only covers stories about our city. Which, last I checked, ain't the world. But, whatever . . . she's *world*-famous, which, I guess, is the reason she spends most of her time locked in her practice room. Gotta practise for the *world*.

Aria's dad, on the other hand – or should I say, on

another *note* (good one, Nee!) – is a locally-loved conductor who tells everyone to call him Maestro. And we all do. Aria says he used to be a big deal, constantly working with professional orchestras, and that's how he met her mother. She also says Maestro decided to cut his work back once she and her sister were born.

These days the most musical Maestro gets is when he conducts elementary school orchestras. Whether it's the spitty little kids playing recorders and kazoos, or the spark-showers squeaking through clarinet solos, tap-tap-tapping on drum pads, and licking and lapping at sax mouthpieces, Maestro believes every kid deserves a chance to make sound, even if it's horrible-sounding. As a matter of fact, to him, real music is all about the melody in mistakes. Expression. Experimentation. Explosion. Which is why he never misses a beat whenever his favourite daughter wants to add what always seems like a giant cymbal crash to their home.

Sometimes that crash comes in the form of requesting that all her food be a certain colour. Once, she would only eat red food for two weeks. Everything red. Apples, spaghetti drenched in sauce, peppers. Another time it was only white foods. But sometimes, her explosions of expression came in the form of asking to have the whole outside of the house painted. Like only a favourite daughter could ask.

But . . . that favourite daughter is *not* Aria. Because she's the oldest. And the title of favourite kid always goes to the baby. Her name's Rosin, but they call her Turtle. She was given that nickname when she was little because of how shy she was. Quick to tuck back into her shell. That is, until she and the rest of the Wrights discovered she had a gift. Turtle can sing. And when I say sing, I mean *sang*. *Sing* sing. Blow. She got one of them voices that can make you sad and mad and happy all at the same time. Like she got an old lady living down in her belly that's seen too much to tell, even though Turtle ain't nothing but nine years old. She's a little thing, too, narrow and navel-height. But got a voice made for weddings, funerals, and movie soundtracks. But only movies about summer or winter, love or heartbreak, or that take place on sprawling landscapes. Because her voice is wide. And tall.

And on top of all this, Turtle also has this special brain

thing called synesthesia. Took me a long time to learn how to pronounce this, and even longer to understand what it means. But basically, for her, it means that when she hears music, she sees colours. Or when she sees colours, she hears music. Or when she . . . I don't know. Her senses get twisted up, and her brain makes her ears do her eyes' job, and her eyes work like ears. Something like that.

So in those moments when Turtle only wants monochromatic meals, it's because she gets fixated on a sound that colour makes. Obsessed with an E-flat, and in her brain, red sounds like E-flat. Fixated on A-sharp, and in her brain, white sounds like A-sharp. And usually, she just eats the one-colour food – eats the sound – and moves on. Except for the times she can't move on. The times when the colour sounds too beautiful to chew. And those are the moments that lead to Maestro painting the whole outside of the house that colour. And because Turtle's seen as special – musically gifted – Mrs Wright's okay with all of it. She *encourages* it.

And Maestro's okay with whatever Mrs Wright's okay with. Also, he's . . . a dad. So he'll do anything for his girls, both of them, regardless of their talents. So when the paint requests come in, he and Aria get to work on the house's new facelift. Because Aria will do anything for her little sister, but really she'll do *whatever* to not be around her mother.

And when you got *that* much going on – Mrs Wright's constant practising, Turtle's specialised musical training and random moments of colour bursts, and Maestro doing . . . pretty much everything else – the Wright residence is almost *never* empty.

But it is this evening.

Turtle has a solo in the school chorus competition. Her first big one. She's been practising all month but made it clear that she didn't want Aria to come, even though Aria is like a one-person pep rally. The type to hype you up from the audience, scream for you like you're famous even when you're barely average. Trust me, I know. At the end of our junior year, I debuted my first short documentary in film class. I say 'debuted,' but really I had no choice because it was the final project and worth a big chunk of our grade. The assignment was loose. Make a film between three and five minutes long using what we'd studied all year: theme, narrative, composition, score, editing. My first idea was to do something about the bingo hall my father owns, where I work three nights a week. Wednesday, Friday, and Saturday. But the thing about bingo players is that some of them got family members who don't know they're out gambling. Folks concerned about their habits, knowing how easy it is for a good night to become a bad month. So them being filmed ain't gon' fly. Plus, I'm no snitch.

With that off the table, I ended up making my movie about . . . cell phones. And I used my cell phone to make it. I thought it was genius. Meta. I got my sister's phone, which is different from mine; my father's phone, which is different from hers; my mother's phone, which is different from his; and my grandmother's phone, which is ancient; and simply filmed each of them as they powered on. Some came on in seconds; others, like Gammy's, took about fifteen minutes. And the soundtrack was just a loop of the old-school busy signal, which I only know about because my mother mimics it whenever she wants me or my sister, Nat, to stop talking to her. Because she's busy. It's a distinct tone, droning and droning and droning. Like the first notes of a song but the beat don't drop.

To me, this film was . . . art. A masterpiece making a statement on the evolution (or lack thereof) of communication. Even though I got a C on it, it was clear by the scrunched-up faces that no one in class really understood my avant-garde brilliance. I guess I didn't communicate it well enough. But Aria, who, by the way, wasn't even in the class, stood in the hallway, watching through the window in the classroom door. You know, the prison window. And when the film was over, she flung the door open and screamed like I'd just won an Oscar.

And got in trouble for it. But didn't care.

Because that's Aria.

So Turtle not wanting her to come to her first chorus competition was basically like asking the captain of the cheerleading squad to not show up for the game. But I get it. Turtle felt like it would be too much pressure if Aria was there and she'd crack or miss a note, even though a crack or missed note from Turtle is better than any songbird's best chirp. Aria agreed to sit this one out, first and foremost because her sister asked, and second-most because she knew this gave us the chance to . . . be together.

Even though we've fooled around at my house a lot, *connecting* definitely can't happen there. Because there's always someone home too. Between my mother, father, sister, and me, someone has to be around to keep an eye on Gammy. She's reached that age where she gets confused every now and then. Sometimes she don't know whose house she's in, and it can hit her in the blink of an eye. It's not too bad yet and doesn't happen too often, but it's something we're all careful about. So one of us is always home. And that's okay, because even if, for whatever reason, I was lucky enough to have the house to myself, and me and Aria decided to do it at Château Neon, I wouldn't have been able to show off and show up, romantic-comedy-style. Bearing gifts. Chicken tenders. Sexy chicken tenders.

I'd thought about bringing flowers. Roses. But I know Aria. Even though she likes flowers, she don't like them more than breaded, deep-fried, misshapen chunks of chicken breast. Especially breaded, deep-fried, misshapen chunks of chicken breast from the bingo hall. Which is where I was coming from. Work.

I'd spent hours down at the hall, minding the suspicious and superstitious bingo players. The newbies and the vets and the unfortunate obsessed. The old men in durags, the young women in bonnets. The wigs that look like hats and the hats that look like wigs. The players who nurse one card at a time, and the others who play half a table's worth. And even though my father don't allow smoking no more – there used to be a designated room – the place still reeks of stale cigarettes.

My job is simple. Usually. Just dole out extra cards to whoever wants them and cash out the winners. But the whole time I was there, my mind was in Aria Land. The distraction was so bad that I messed up Mrs Monihan's winnings three times before getting it right.

'You okay, Neon?' Mrs Monihan asked, her eyes narrowed into the shape of concern. 'Because you acting funny, and ain't nothing funny about messing up my cash.'

And I wanted to respond, *No, Mrs Monihan, I'm not okay. Because as soon as I leave here, I'm going to hop on the bus and ride to the other side of town to my girlfriend's house. And know what we're going to do when I get there?* But then I looked at all the good luck charms lined up in front of her – a bottle of pink nail polish, a pair of sunglasses, an old car key, a frayed book, a Barbie doll, a figurine of a dog, a tiny skull, a quarter, a coffee mug, a movie ticket, a corkscrew, and a creased-up funeral program – and decided to just count out the money again.

For the fourth time.

Mrs Monihan, the queen of the blonde finger waves and the black finger wave, hadn't hit all night. Lost every round after dumping money into extra cards to up her chances. But finally, on the last game – the big game – she hit. It was the blackout round, which meant in order to win, every number on the card had to be called. It had the largest payout, and when Mrs Monihan *Bingo'd!*, she stood up and sang it in a dramatic falsetto as if Neon Bingo were a concert hall. And this was a concert. For yodelers. And everybody else groaned, partially because of her winning and partially because of her singing.

By the time I got over to her, she was kissing each of her

trinkets, her parade of lucky charms, one by one. They each had something to do with her deceased husband. Their first movie date. His car. The polish she knew he liked on her nails. I'd heard the stories about him over the years, but when you hit big after losing so much, you think more about reimbursement than reminiscing.

After kissing trinket twelve, Mrs Monihan jumped up and gave *me* a big kiss on the cheek too.

'And also, thank *you*, good luck charm number thirteen!'

'What makes you think I'm one of your good luck charms, Mrs Monihan?' I asked, trying to resist wiping the wet from my cheek.

'Because this place is *named* after you!' she said. Then, poking my shoulder, added, 'Plus, *you* sold me that card.'

'But I sold lots of people cards,' I replied. 'Even sold you a bunch of duds that ain't play out for you.'

'Yeah, but this was the game that counted! Plus, all these other folks in here ain't got the power of Ronald,' she said, pointing at the charms. 'It's a combination, a recipe, and you part of that. That's why I only play here when *you* work. You got power over this place.'

This was a gambler's lie. I was used to them.

When Ms Whitestone wins, she swears it's because her right leg was crossed over her left leg. Except for when she loses. Then the reason for losing is because her left leg wasn't crossed over her right leg. Or whenever Mr Stallworth wins, he swears it's because he said his prayers at the perfect volume before coming into the hall. He does this in his car in the parking lot, and if he doesn't win, it's because he wasn't loud enough, and God couldn't hear him. And if he was loud and still don't win, he says it's because God don't like to be yelled at. So when Mrs Monihan told me she'd won because of some power I had over the place, I knew not to take it seriously.

I got no power over the bingo hall, even though it's named after me. And even though it's kinda cool to have my name on a building – *Neon* in neon – it don't necessarily represent who I am. At least not completely. I mean, the hall is a plain room with old-school foldable tables. It could easily be any multipurpose room. Or lunchroom. Or church basement. That part I can relate to. I can be many things. Anything. Many anythings. However, I don't feel like I'm a home for gamblers. A place for folks to come blow their bread and sometimes ruin their lives while feasting on chicken tenders and chewy pizza. Or tots. Or oversalted but delicious crinkle-cut fries. Or potato salad that we always sell out of even though no one ever knows who's making it.

I'd like to think I'm a little more than that. A safer bet with better options.

'If you say so, Mrs Monihan,' I said, finally getting the count right. Five thousand. Fifty one-hundred-dollar bills.

'How your grandma doin'?' Mrs Monihan asked, recounting the cash in her head while conversing at the same time. A pro.

'Still knockin',' I said. Mrs Monihan nodded, happy to hear that.

'Tell her I miss seeing her in here and that she should come check on us sometime.'

'You know she not leaving that dog.'

'Yeah, I know. Trust me, I lost Ronald almost twenty years ago, so I get needing what you need to get by.' Mrs Monihan shook her head, trying to shake grief from her hair like dandruff. 'Tell her to bring the damn dog with her. What's its name again?' She paused her count, licked her thumb, then resumed.

'Denzel Jeremy Washington.'

'That's right, Denzel Jeremy Washington. And you gotta say the whole name every time, right?'

'Yes, ma'am.'

'Well, shit, Denzel Jeremy Washington might be her good luck charm,' she said. 'Especially mixed with you!' I laughed, knowing Gammy would never bring that dog to the bingo hall because my father would never let a dog in here, especially *that* dog. Too much barking. 'Anyway, what about that girlfriend of yours? How she doin'?'

Mrs Monihan, now done with the recount, handed me a hundred-dollar tip, which almost felt like payment for her minding my business.

Aria's fine. So fine, *fine* don't even seem right. Never has. Matter fact, I'd spent half my shift thinking about a word that was better than *fine* so I could pay Aria a different compliment when I saw her. *Beautiful* felt like something an old man would say. *Gorgeous* felt like something a dirty old man would say. She deserved something more. And honestly, she deserved something other than chicken tenders too. If I could've afforded it or knew where to get it, there would've been some caviar on those chicken tenders. I've never had caviar, but I knew this was a caviar kind of night. A candlelight kind of night. A cabernet kind of night. Never had that either, but if I had some, I would've drank it on this night, for sure.

'Aria's fine,' I replied to Mrs Monihan. 'I'm actually gonna go see her later.'

Mrs Monihan looked me up and down. Just a quick once-over, as if she could tell by the way I was standing that I was on the brink of something life-changing. She grinned.

'Well, you make sure you tell her I said hello.'

After Mrs Monihan took her money and ran, I quickly put the order in, for chicken tenders and fries, before Big Boy, the fry cook, dumped the grease for the night. Then I beelined to the bathroom, not to pee but to freshen up. But ain't no place bad for a birdbath like the bathroom of a bingo hall. Especially when Mr Stanfield, another one of the hall's regulars, was in the stall, struggle-humming the theme song to Star Wars while dumping his gut, which sounded like pain. And smelled like . . . pain. So much pain, I feared it would get caught in my clothes. Which would defeat the purpose of trying to freshen up. Nonetheless, the situation was the situation.

At the sink, I pumped the soap dispenser, rubbed my hands together for lather, then eased them down my pants, scrubbing and cupping, cupping and scrubbing, no longer than five seconds. Just enough to dial down the day-funk. Then I washed the suds from my palms and repeated the process with just water for the crotch rinse.

'You ain't jerkin' off in the sink, is yuh, son?' Mr Stanfield said from the stall, a sweet concern in his voice that made the moment ten times weirder.

'What? No! *What?*' In the mirror, I caught Mr Stanfield's eye peering at me through the crack between the stall door and its frame.

'Then what yuh doin'?'

'I ain't doing nothing,' I said, zipping up and bombing from the bathroom.

• • • •

I was still soggy in the pants by the time the chicken tenders order was up. Fries on the bottom, tenders on top, wrapped in foil, then a box, finished off in a plastic bag, which made them easier to hold as I stood waiting at the bus stop outside the hall. I stared at the car dealership across the street, the fluorescent graffiti advertising the DAZZLING DEALS written huge on the showroom windows. I glanced back at the bingo hall. Nothing on the windows. Nothing dazzling about it.

I was still a little soggy when the bus came. And after twenty minutes of watching videos on my phone, scrolling from clip to clip, I was a little less soggy by the time I got off. I hoped what was left of the damp would dry on my walk to Aria's house, especially since it was a warmer spring night than usual. May can be tricky.

Aria lives two blocks from the stop, in a neighbourhood that's way quieter than mine. It's one of them neighbourhoods that's less of a neighbourhood and more of a 'community.' Streetlights are brighter, houses bigger, grass so green that it seems just as green at night. Every house looks the same. Each the colour of graham crackers. And they all look like the people who live in them might eat graham crackers. For breakfast. For lunch. For dinner and nighttime snack. Because this is definitely a community where people eat nighttime snacks. Wouldn't surprise me at all if there's even a person *named* Graham laid up on a beige sofa in one of these mini-mansions. Eating nighttime snacks.

Before I knew it, I was standing at Aria's front door – 873 Kingman Park Drive – the only house that stood out because of its pink paint. A spark in the dark. A blam in the blah.

I approached the door knocker, the whole note (that looked like an eye) made of brass. I took a moment and just stood there staring at it before finally working up the courage to use it.

I lifted it, slammed it down. Lifted it, slammed it down. *Twice should be enough*, I thought. But just in case, I lifted and slammed once more.

'Okay, okay, okay,' I muttered, rocking back and forth from heel to toe, over and over again, trying to hand-iron

the wrinkles from my shirt. Wasn't working, but worth a try. Then came the soft thump of Aria's feet.

'Okay, okay, okay!' she said from the other side. 'No need to knock the door down.'

Then, the click of the lock unlocking.

And there she was. In sweatpants and a T-shirt, her hair snatched back into a ponytail. Ankle socks with ballies on the back.

'You know we got a doorbell, right?' To her, the door knocker was just decoration.

'And you know I got chicken tenders, right?' I replied, holding out the bag. She lit up.

'I swear, you the best boyfriend ever. Don't let nobody ever tell you different,' she said, taking the bag and kissing me.

'Pretty low bar if chicken tenders can get me a compliment like that,' I said, following her into the house. She set the food on the kitchen table next to a notepad full of scribbles and scratch-outs.

'What's all this?' I asked, pointing at the yellow paper. 'I know you. There's no way you're still doing homework this late.'

'Of course not. This is actually yearbook stuff. Feels like we running out of time.'

'Tell me about it,' I said. And for a tick, just a tick, there was sadness between us. Sadness that comes from the unknown. There's, like, the graduation stage, and then there's graduating from this stage to another. And we don't know what that stage holds for us. So, every now and then, there's a pinch. But luckily it has a quick release.

'The Big Day's almost here. Which means we got, like, a month to get this thing done. It's crunch time.' Aria snapped us out of it. Snapped us back into the moment.

Me, Aria, and four of our friends make up the yearbook club, which we don't like calling a club. We call it a staff. Sounds more professional. More important. Because, to us, it *is* important. I mean, it's the last document of our class's time together, and even though we hate to talk about it, it might even be the last document of the six of us all together. Who knows? Not us. Who cares? Well . . . we do. So we've all signed up for different responsibilities thanks to the club – I mean, *staff* – advisor, Mr Sanchez.

At first, I was going to be the photographer but realised

we didn't need one because these days, everybody's a photographer. So instead of taking pictures, we just created an email address for our classmates to send in the photos they've snapped on their phones throughout the year. Easy. Because everyone has at least ten million selfies. With that taken care of, I decided to do something different for the graduating class: make a short video of each senior, asking them to describe high school in three words. This is because, for the first time, our yearbook is going to be online. So these videos will be viewable forever.

Aria's job is to create all the senior superlatives. And because Aria is Aria, she's been obsessed with coming up with some unique categories for our class to vote on.

'Voting has to start soon, and I'm still trying to get 'em all nailed down,' she said, eyeing the notepad. 'You were supposed to be helping me. *Ahem.*'

'I am. I will. I'm ready.' I saluted. 'What you got?'

'Well, just before you came, I was playing around with *Most Likely to Get Famous for No Reason at All.*'

'*Gotta* be you,' I poked.

'*What?!* No. That's definitely Dodie. That fool's gonna

stumble into stardom. I don't know when or how, but watch. It's just his luck.' Aria returned her attention to the chicken tenders and started digging through the layers of plastic, cardboard, and foil before reaching her well-protected treasure. Still warm.

She put her nose in first, inhaled the aroma.

'And you'll definitely get voted in for *Most Likely to Win an Oscar*,' she said.

She reached in, grabbed a tender.

'Me?'

'Uh-huh.' Her face was unflinching. She meant it.

'And the bar has now officially hit the floor,' I teased. 'If only I could provide chicken tenders to all of Hollywood, maybe they'll lower their standards too.'

Aria had almost bitten into the tender but paused.

'Don't get it twisted. My standards ain't low. I just actually love chicken tenders. And you know that. So the way I see it, to love me the way I love to be loved is *true* love,' she said. 'Therefore, the bar is actually set pretty high.' She flashed a look – the one that usually comes after *Don't get it twisted* – and finally took a bite.

'I praise well thy wit,' I said, in my best *tah-tah* voice.

'Oh, listen to *you*, Mr Canterbury,' she taunted before sitting and taking another bite and another, each followed by a dunk in the honey mustard.

'Please. Them five words are pretty much where I begin and end with that book,' I scoffed. We'd been assigned *The Canterbury Tales* in English class, and I'd never known reading could feel so much like math. 'Anyway, how was Turtle before she left? Nervous?'

I slid my wallet from my back pocket before taking a seat. Set it on the table like it was a leather stone. It was my grandfather's and messes up the way I sit, but I carry it everywhere I go. Kinda like *my* own good luck charm. *My* bingo magnet.

'Not really. I'm just bummed she gotta listen to our parents fight for the two hours it takes to get there, and the two hours back. Not to mention she has to deal with my father cranking and clicking his disposable camera all night.'

'Oof.' I groaned. 'That's a lot.'

'Yeah, and I'm also bummed that no matter how well Turtle does tonight, her voice will never add up to mine,' Aria joked, straight-faced.

'Oh *really*?'

'Of course. We all know that's the actual reason she ain't want me to come.' Then Aria broke into song. Didn't bother clearing the chicken from her throat or nothing. Just went for it. And it was horrible. Absolutely terrible. Not a single note hit or carried. Not even by accident. See, even though Aria comes from a musical family, she's the only member who don't have no music in her. Not even a hum. And that's the second reason she was *Least Likely to Be the Favourite Daughter*.

'Wow' was all I could muster.

'My voice ain't warmed up, that's all,' Aria explained.

I shot her bail. 'Or maybe my ears ain't warmed up.'

'Right, it's probably just your ears. Too small to recognise perfect pitch.'

'Too bad they ain't just a *little* . . . bit . . . smaller.' I folded the tops of my ears down. 'At least you sound better than that dog you love so much.'

'Oh, you got jokes? Okay, well . . .' And then she broke into song again. This time howling like a sick dog about the chicken tenders, asking me if I wanted some. *'Chicken tenders, golden and crispy and deep-fried with lovvvvvvvve. Deep-fried with lovvvvvvvve.* I said, *Deep-fried with lovvvvvvvve.*'

'I got you, I got you. Deep-fried with love.' I laughed, shook my head. 'But I don't want none.'

'Fine. But I *know* you want some fries. You *always* want fries. You the *Most Likely to Come Back in Your Next Life as a French Fry*.'

She slid the box over to me and grabbed her pad to write down that ridiculous idea. And she was right. I did always want fries. Who don't? They're my favourite food because they're the best food. Simple and versatile and, to me, perfect for every occasion.

'And when I do come back as a fry, hopefully I'll share a box with you, the *Most Likely to Come Back as a Chicken Tender*.' Aria smiled. Nailed it. 'Only difference is, I'd probably get eaten by Denzel Jeremy Washington.' Aria frowned.

'Aww, don't say that. He would never,' she cooed. 'How's my baby doing, anyway?'

Her *baby*. A pet name only reserved for that mutt. I was many other things, but never her *baby*.

'He's fine. Fed. Walked. Loved.' I pinched a fry from the box. 'Also, he still ugly and still mean to me despite how much I do for him.'

'Well, you mean to me despite how much I do for you, so . . . it's even, right?'

'Please. I ain't never mean to you. Couldn't be if I tried. That's how we ended up here in the first place,' I said, taking a few more fries. 'By the way, Mrs Monihan told me to tell you hi. She won the big bingo tonight. Made enough money to probably last the next two months, but she'll probably blow it all at the hall tomorrow.'

'Maybe.' Aria shrugged. 'I mean, everybody's got their something, right?'

She took another bite of chicken. I shoved the fries in my mouth.

'Oh yeah?' I masked my chew.

'Yep.'

'Well . . . what's *your* something?'

Aria swallowed, dabbed the mustard from the corners of her mouth. Picked up a fry and pointed it at me as if it were a greasy magic wand.

'You,' she said. 'You my something.'

It had been a long time since I'd felt awkward around her. A long time. Usually when Aria said stuff like this, something sopping with slick and game, I'd fire right back, because my sister had done a pretty good job at equipping me with an answer to everything, because our father had done a pretty good job at equipping her with an answer to everything. And if I ain't have no comeback, I'd just lean in for a kiss, because that's the ultimate default. When in doubt, smooch it out. But this evening, I had nothing. No comeback, no get-up-and-lean-in. No nothing. Just sat there with my tongue turned into mashed potatoes, staring at Aria gnawing on those chicken tenders, wondering what it was about chicken tenders, anyway. They require so much work to get down, which means they not even really all that tender. And the ones that come from the bingo hall are always overfried, because they're refried every time somebody makes an order. And if no one makes an order, they're saved until someone does. Maybe my dad thinks hot oil kills all germs. Or that folks are already gambling, anyway, so what's one more risk? Aria's eaten at least a thousand of them since we've been together, and she ain't mutated yet. She ain't even been queasy. I've had a few – only on the fresh days, and none tonight, and yet it was me who all of a sudden felt sick. It was me who felt like my throat was a little blocked, as if the chicken-fried sawdust was lodged somewhere along the runway between apple and sternum, which wasn't no distance at all. I'm a short-neck boy. Not like Aria, who got enough to lay her head on her own shoulder. Which she does sometimes when she looks at me. Which she was doing just then.

'What you thinking about?' she asked.

'Right now?'

'No, twenty seconds from now,' she razzed. 'Of course right now.'

'You.'

She waited a few beats. Smirked.

'Okay, so . . . what you thinking about *now*?' she asked.

I swallowed her flirt, let it sizzle in my stomach before responding.

'Us.'

And just twenty-four hours before that . . .

State your name.

My name's Pendarvis Brown.

And how would you describe high school in three words?

Easy. Hard. Whatever.

State your name.

Ronisha Webb.

And how would you describe high school in three words?

Only three words?

Yes, Ronisha. Only three words.

Hmmm, if I can only use three, I guess I gotta go with What the—

Ronisha.

What? I was gonna say hell.

Hell still counts as a cuss word.

No, I really mean school is hell. Like the opposite of heaven. Hell.

Oh . . . um, okay.

State your name.

You know my name.

State your name.

Dodie.

Your full name.

Big Dodie.

Come on, Dodie.

Okay, okay. Dodie Parr, superstar.

And how would you describe high school in three words?

I was in my room trying to block out Denzel Jeremy Washington's metronome of barking while flipping through the videos I'd recorded earlier in the day, now downloaded onto my laptop. The clips were of my classmates delivering their three-word descriptions of high school. This, of course, was a way for me to block out the fact that I had homework, which wasn't nearly as interesting or as entertaining as seventeen-year-olds trying not to cuss in a yearbook video. That was Mr Sanchez's one rule. No cussing. He said that if anyone got too spicy, he would pull the plug on the whole idea of a digital yearbook. So most of the videos were of tongue-bitten teens, each trying to find the right words to replace the real right words that Mr Sanchez would've seen as wrong words.

I hadn't recorded mine yet, but if, for some reason, I had to do it in that moment, my three words probably would've been about the one thing I was constantly trying to avoid. Homework. *Homework is trash.* And I have a theory about why it even exists. I've heard teachers say that when they get home, they have to grade tests and quizzes, read essays and figure out report cards and all that. So since *they* have to take work home, they make sure *we* have to take work home too. And the reason that's dumb is because all that does is add more work to the work *they* gotta take home. So basically, I'm saying that whenever teachers try to punish us, they just end up punishing themselves more.

Which means homework actually serves no one. Trash. But I had it nonetheless.

In this case, it was English homework. And just when I thought I'd put together the perfect cocktail of distraction, a bigger one fell in my lap. Well, actually, it sat on my bed. But first it knocked on my door.

Two medium and a drag, my sister's knock. Everybody in my family's got one. My father's is four soft, followed by one medium. He typically uses his fingertips. My mother's is three medium with knuckles, then three medium with tips. For balance, she says. And Gammy's is one medium, which is all she can muster at her age.

'Hmm?' I groaned from the bed. There was no reason for me to give Nat a formal *Come in*.

'You dressed?' Nat asked, peeking.

'Of course I'm dressed. I live with three other nosy people.' It came out sharper than I meant it. Homework does that to me.

'You talk about us like we spies,' Nat said, now pushing the door open.

'You talk about y'all like y'all not,' I shot back.

'*Damn*. Somebody's in a mood, huh? Don't act like we don't all respect your space, Nee.' Nat closed the door behind her.

'Respect? That's funny. You know why Ma's knock is the longest?' And before Nat could answer, I stormed on. 'Because she thinks that if she knocks long, it'll give me enough time to get decent, since she's coming in whether I want her to or not. She even be in here when I'm not home. Looking around for . . . whatever.'

'I'll talk to her. That's . . . ridiculous,' Nat grumped, sweeping sneakers out of the way with her foot.

'Hold on, hold on,' I cautioned. 'Before you sit, do you know anything about *The Canterbury Tales*?' I folded my arms as if I were waiting to determine if my sister deserved a seat.

'Of course I do.' Nat eased down on the bed. The edge of it. But only after brushing it with her palm in case there was some sort of leftover little-brother debris.

'"The Franklin's Tale"?' I held up the book, which had been lying next to me, butterflied and face down. Before I gave up and started combing through the senior videos,

I'd been reading the first line of the prologue over and over again. No matter how many times I read it, it wasn't making sense.

'Oh, nope,' Nat said. '"The Knight's Tale" is my jam.'

'Probably because it's the first story in the book.'

'*And* . . . as far as I got.' Nat yikes'd her face and shrugged.

'Well . . . I'll just ask Savion. Thanks for nothing.' I set the book back on the bed. 'Seriously, what's the point of having an older sister if you can't help me cheat? Ain't these the same classes you took in school? It's not like we learning something different.'

'First of all, yes, I took this class, but I had a different teacher, so the assignments were different. Second of all, if you think I remember everything from high school, you've lost your mind.'

'Or maybe you've lost yours.'

'Fair. Maybe. But I know better than to question the type of big sister I am. Especially since I'm the type that teaches her little brother not to mess up his friendships fighting over girls.'

'I don't even know what—' *That has to do with anything* is what I was going to say before she cut in.

'That's from "The Knight's Tale."' She bounced her eyebrows and tapped her forehead. 'See? Ain't lost all of it.'

'Whatever.'

'I'm also the type of sister who lets her brother sneak-drive her car late at night even though he don't have a licence.'

'I got a learner's,' I snipped.

'But not a *licence*. And you know *why* I did it? Just so he can go fumble around with his girlfriend.' Nat went into know-it-all mode, which is basically big-sister mode, and made the face to match. 'And, on top of that, kept it a secret.'

'Okay, you got that one. But—'

'Oh, I'm not done.' Nat slipped her hand under her butt, slid her phone from her back pocket. 'I'm *also* the kind of big sister who wants to show some pictures of what I worked on for *you* today at the shop.' Nat unlocked her phone, passed it to me. On the screen was an image of a metal mould of . . . something.

'What's . . . this?'

'That is the casting mould for Aria's door knocker.'

Suddenly the image dented into the mould became clear.

'Ugh,' I yuck'd. 'That damn dog's face.'

'Yep,' Nat confirmed. 'It probably won't be ready by graduation, but it'll definitely be good to go before she leaves for college. She'll have a Natalie Benton original, courtesy of you.' She poked my nose the way she used to do when she first started working in the shop. Back when she would smear a black smudge on it. Sister pranks. Workshop jokes. Door-knocker-maker humour.

See, besides my dad being in the bingo business, my mom's side of the family is in the door-knocker business. Four generations deep. My great-grandfather started it a long, long time ago as a way to give Black people and poor people some front-door fashion. A bow tie for the abode. An ornament on the door of what were sometimes run-down establishments as a way to say ain't no run-down folks inside. I never got to meet my great-grandfather, but I was told this story by my grandfather, who I called Grandy.

Grandy inherited the shop after his father passed.

Grandy is also who made it an actual business and named it Wednesday's Door Knockers. A couple years ago, after Grandy died, my mother took over the shop and hired my sister, who will probably inherit it someday. Even though nobody really needs a door knocker no more because . . . doorbells. Even though a lot of people really don't even use doorbells no more because . . . cell phones. But still. Decoration is decoration, like a brass whole note (that looks like an eye) on a pink front door.

A few months ago I'd asked Nat to make Aria a special door knocker to take with her to college. Something to hang on her dorm-room door. A small thing to remind her of home. I wanted it to be chicken tenders, but they don't translate to brass very well. Then I thought about doing a different take on the door knocker that hangs on the door at her house. The whole note. But make it a quarter note. One beat to represent her . . . as her. But I thought it might hit *too* close to home. Then I thought maybe my face would be a cool gift, but both my mother and sister made it clear to me that that wasn't a good look. As if Denzel Jeremy Washington's mug was somehow better.

I'm cuter than him. I don't care what nobody says.

'For the hammer part, I'm gonna make a long tongue!' Nat was way too excited about this. I mean, to me, it was a door knocker. Sure, it was for Aria, but still just a door knocker. But for Nat, who'd been apprenticing for years, this was her first big project as a door-knocker maker.

'It's cool. I mean . . . I think she's gonna love it, which is all that matters,' I said. Which was all I could think of saying because that picture, which was going to eventually be a glossy hunk of metal, was a symbol of an inevitable – and hopefully temporary – separation between Aria and me. Because she was going to college. She hadn't made a choice about which school she was going to yet, but Aria had options. Lots of options. And most of them were out of state.

We don't talk about it. We tried. But we can't. So we don't. And for now, that's fine.

Me, I'm not going to college. At least not regular college. And that's fine too. School ain't really my thing, not because I'm not smart, but because nobody can convince me *The Canterbury Tales* is somehow going to help me pay rent. Or that me being able to read Middle English – *hast* and *thou* and *thy* – will for sure make me a better fit for film school. Which is what I *really* want to do. Film school. But not right away because I gotta get money to afford that, and I'm pretty sure 'The Franklin's Tale' ain't gonna make me more hirable. Not to mention, I'm already hired. Was born hired because I'm going to work at the bingo hall. I'll learn the business, stack my bread for tuition, and maybe even buy a camera before studying how to make a movie. A forreal movie. Who knows, my first flick might be *about* the bingo hall. Not the players, but the bingo business itself. And after it becomes a hit – maybe an Oscar, but at least a Golden Globe – I might even use some of my money to open up a whole casino with a movie theatre in it. And on the sign, high up in the sky, will be my face like a beacon calling out to Aria, reminding her where the jackpot is. Bingo!

But a door knocker of a dog will have to do for now.

'Yeah, I think she'll like it too!' Nat was saying while glancing down at the floor. 'You know what else she might like? If you . . . maybe think about . . . cleaning up in here—'

'Nat, what you want?' I know my sister. She does everything she can to not come into my room. Unless she wants something.

'I told you. I came to show you the mould.'

'Okay, I saw it, so—'

'*And* . . . to talk about tomorrow,' she finally admitted. 'Sorry. But . . . yeah. How you feeling about it?' And just then her phone rang. And without having to say who it was, I knew it was a boy. One of the many. Had to be, because she grinned.

'Pause for the cause,' she said, springing from the bed. 'Give me three minutes, then we'll get to it.'

The *it* Nat was asking about was mine and Aria's. Our *it*. Our . . . moment. And the only reason Nat was asking about it was because I'd told her about it. Because she's . . . Nat. I guess a better way to put it is to say Nat ain't just my older sister; she my older best friend. My older homegirl – a literal *home*girl – who has always had deep-enough pockets to hold my secrets. To walk with them without risk of them weighing her down, or falling out. I told her months ago what Aria and me were planning. Then told her again a week ago. Then told her again yesterday. So she was asking because it was on her mind – I made sure of it. Plus, she of all people knew it was on my mind too, and the distractions – the dog barking, the videos, even the homework – were really just ways to not think about it so much.

With Nat now on the other side of the door – a three-minute mental-health break for me – I lay back on the bed and turned the book of Chaucer's words into a tent of *hithers* and *thithers* over my head. I stretched my legs out, accidentally kicking the laptop, apparently, and, more specifically, the space bar. Because a few seconds later . . . Dodie's voice. Again.

Okay, okay. Dodie Parr, superstar.

And how would you describe high school in three words?

How would I describe *Dodie Parr* in three words? Not real sure. Or maybe *those* are the words I would use to describe him at any given time. Sometimes he's *not*. Sometimes *real*. Sometimes *sure*. All the time, he's one of the most ridiculous humans I've ever known. Tall dude. Too tall for high school, especially to not be an athlete.

And especially to be a singer. Not a singer like Turtle, who will probably grow up to be an opera star. And not even a singer like Aria, which is a . . . bad singer. Dodie is the singer, the *lead* singer, of a punk band. Which means Dodie is a screamer. And he got a nose ring. And a tattoo of a cheeseburger on his hand, because the name of his band is Knuckle Sandwich. And he always got on sunglasses, even in school, which means he's always being told to take them off, which means he's got an ever-growing list of lies he launches at teachers and administrators explaining why he don't have no choice but to wear them. From dilated pupils to triple pink eye, even though he only has two eyes. He rocks a bald head, and a bald face, and got bald tires on his bucket – a red Honda – he affectionately refers to as 'Cherry.'

One of the moments he could be described as *sure* is every morning when he picks me up for school. This morning was no different. Dodie (and Cherry) pulled up at seven like usual. He honked the horn, which turned Denzel Jeremy Washington into a siren of barks.

'Ma, I'm gone!' I grabbed my backpack and headed for the door.

'Have a good day!' Ma yelled from the bathroom.

Weekday mornings are all the same. My dad sleeps late because the bingo hall stays open until midnight, and by the time he counts the money and locks everything up, he usually doesn't make it home until one in the morning. Two on the busy nights. So he's always snoozing when I'm leaving for school. Pillow over his head to mute the mayhem of the morning.

Gammy, on the other hand, is awake before Jesus. And dressed as if she's expecting him to stop by for breakfast. She's always sitting on the couch, dog on lap, coffee in hand, watching an old movie. This one called *Mississippi Masala* is her favourite, but I've never seen it all the way through because she always watches it in the morning, while waiting for someone – usually my mother – to walk with her down to the cemetery to visit her husband. That is . . . until the day Jesus *actually* shows up to do it. This is an everyday thing.

Ma spends forever in the bathroom in the morning, even though she knows Gammy is waiting for her. She takes a shower. Then takes a bath. Then takes another shower. She says it's important to ease into the day.

And Nat usually stays at one of her boyfriends' (who are not her boyfriends) houses and comes home right after Gammy and Ma have already left for the daily graveyard visit. This is to avoid their judgy eyes and those nosy noses that always wrinkle with curiosity and suspicion.

Dodie honked again, rushing me.

'Bye, Gammy,' I said, smooching her forehead. She could barely hear me over all the barking. Then I was out the door.

When I plopped down on the passenger side of Cherry, I was greeted first by Dodie's sly grin.

'Mornin',' I said. Dodie turned down his music.

'Good morning to *you*,' he replied. 'How you feeling?'

'I'm feeling like you need to give me your three-word description,' I said, straight to the point.

'Of me? Oh, that's easy.' Dodie reached for the rearview mirror, turned it toward himself to check his face, then acted shocked by what he saw. 'Beautiful Black boy.'

'You know what I'm talkin' about, D.' I reached back and grabbed the seat belt, yanked it across my chest.

'Okay. How 'bout this? You got my word that I'm

gonna drive slow enough for you to not have to strap yourself in like that. You got my word, you won't die. You got my word that I'm the best driver you know. Boom. Three words.'

'Safety first,' I murmured. 'And that's not what I'm talking about. I'm talking about your yearbook video. You never said what your three words to describe high school would—'

'Sorry,' Dodie interrupted while turning up the radio. Guitars. Drums. Screams. 'I can't hear you!' Dodie put his cruddy Honda in reverse. Denzel Jeremy Washington barked a cuss-out in the living room window as we backed onto the street and pulled away.

I gazed out at the neighbourhood I'd grown up in. This old Black suburb with no sign or gate, just a name that was nowhere to be seen but everyone knew was Paradise Hill. The fresh-blooming trees that used to be bases for hide-and-seek. The jagged sidewalks I'd raced on. The oil-stained streets I'd learned to ride a bike on. The park I had my first fight in, Nat in my corner, cheering me on. The asphalt burns that still scar my elbows and knees and tell the stories of my fuckups, get-ups, and stand-ups. The junk-drawer mix of neighbours who all know each other, some through friendship, others through enemy-ship, but there's no beef a barbecue grill can't cure. Neighbours whose sons used to be my heroes, and, more importantly, whose daughters used to be my crushes. My almost-first kisses never made real just because I was too shy to say or do anything. Most of those girls still live around here but are more like the sister type now. Not a sister like Nat but sister-*ish*. And none of them can believe I got a girlfriend. Me, nervous Neon.

I rolled my window down, let some of Dodie's cheap cologne out, the same cologne my grandfather used to wear. But Dodie rolled the window back up.

'I need air,' I confessed.

'I understand that, but I need your ear!' Dodie screamed over the music.

'My ear for . . .' I turned the dial on the radio to lower the volume. 'My ear for what?' As soon as I took my hand off the knob, Dodie reached for it to turn it back up. Then he grabbed his phone.

'I want you to hear something. Knuckle Sandwich's new shit.'

'I'm good,' I deflected. I wasn't trying to be mean. I was down to hear it, but not until we weren't . . . moving. As long as Dodie had to search his phone for the song while also driving, I didn't want to hear nothing.

'No, no, you gotta hear it, man. Definitely our best yet,' he said, scrolling and scrolling, until I took the phone from him, annoyed.

'I'll find it for you. Just . . . drive.'

Even though I'd now taken over music duty, he still hadn't taken his eyes off me. Worst driver ever.

'The name of the song is "Empty the Clip."'

'"Empty the Clip"?' The confusion in my voice came from the fact that Dodie was the furthest thing from street.

'"Empty the Clip,"' Dodie confirmed, nodding, already satisfied. Then, noticing my concern, added, 'Relax. It's a love song.'

I tapped the cell phone screen, and the song started playing. The bass heavy and fast. A scratchy guitar came in, shrieking. And then came Dodie's voice. Like I said, his singing voice is more of a tire screech.

I won't lie. I tried to ignore the song. Not because I didn't want to support Dodie. I did. And I do. I go to his shows and jump around and all that. But to ride in the car with him on our way to school and to see him singing his heart, lungs, and whole stomach out was just awkward. It was like he was throwing up . . . sound.

I tried to roll the window down midsong, but Dodie had locked the windows, slick. And two minutes later, when the song finished, he asked, 'What you think? It's a hit, right?'

'I mean, maybe.' I mustered up some encouragement. 'But I just don't . . . get it.'

'Get what?'

'What it's about.'

'What you mean? You ain't hear it?' Dodie snatched his phone out the cupholder I'd set it in and restarted the tune.

This time I cut the whole radio off. The whole damn thing.

'We don't have to listen to it again. Just tell me what it's about,' I insisted.

'Emptying your clip.' Dodie glanced at me and then realised I wasn't picking up what he was putting down. 'You don't know what emptying your clip is?'

Dodie stopped at the red light at the end of the block. Looked at me, which became me looking at me through the reflection in his shades. Then he tilted the frames down so that he could make sure I saw the disappointment in his eyes.

'Look, I know I said it was a love song. But really, it's a lesson song. Listen to this lyric: *If you don't want a faster date, then it's best you masturbate.*' Dodie added some vibrato on the end of that one, for extra effect. Slapped my shoulder a few times for *extra* extra effect. '*You* know, *you* know!' And all I could think about was whether or not the hand he was using was . . . the hand he used. Which, by the way, was funny, because Dodie always swore he never jerked off because he never needed to.

I wanted to call him on it. But I didn't. No need.

The thing about Dodie is, this is who he was all the time.

A lover in his own mind. But I ain't never known Dodie to be with nobody, except for Lana Spuddy. And that's new. And he too scared of her daddy to try no punk mess. All that screaming and jumping around ain't happening. But Dodie talks big. Talks like he's been with everybody and their mama.

Been like that since middle school. Dodie moved to Paradise Hill halfway through seventh grade, and when he arrived, he was super shy. So, since I was a shy boy too, I basically took him under my wing. I'm kidding. At that point, my wings were too short to shelter anybody. Plus, he wasn't like any other bird I'd ever seen. Dodie was featherless. Completely bald, yes, even back then. And if it wasn't for what he said on his first day when Mr Mercer made us all go around the room introducing ourselves, I would've thought he just had funny fashion sense. You know, trying to be different or something.

'Okay, Dodie, now it's your turn,' Mr Mercer said, prompting him to do what the rest of us had already done, which was to say our names and something interesting about ourselves. My fun fact was that I was . . .

uncomfortable . . . around dogs. It was the only thing I could think of. The bingo hall wasn't interesting to me yet. Neither was the door-knocker shop. Plus, both felt like things I could be teased about, and if there's one thing I'd learned back then, it was that the only thing worse than being teased is being teased about your parents. But dogs? Plenty of people got problems with dogs.

Dodie stood up.

'My name's Dodie Parr,' he said, shifting his weight from one leg to the other. 'And I got alopecia, which is why I don't have no hair. So . . . yeah.'

'Well, Dodie, that makes two of us,' Mr Mercer said, patting his bald spot. 'But mine isn't from alopecia. It's from *old*-opecia.' No one laughed. Not even Dodie. Because in the seventh grade, a bald head wasn't a joke. It was joke bait. 'Anyway, um . . . welcome. We're happy to have you.'

I don't actually remember how me and Dodie met, even though Dodie always says I came up to him and told him I ain't have no friends either, which is a lie because I definitely had friends. Not a lot, but I had some. However, what I do remember is how he told me he didn't need friends because he had girls. Even though he didn't. Told me he'd come to this school because he got kicked out his old school for getting caught getting a blow job in the back of the school bus. And I wasn't the only person he told that to. It was practically the second fun fact about him and would've been the first – the one he would've proclaimed in his introduction – had this not been school. Knowing Dodie, he would've written it across his head in permanent marker if he could've.

Thing is, no one believed him. Matter fact, I distinctly remember our class's designated rich girl, Bria Crestlake, roasting him, telling everybody that she thought all that girl did was kiss Dodie on the cheek, which would've equaled a blow job because his bald head looked like a dick. Literally. Like a penis. And Dodie's response was, 'How you know what a dick look like?'

And she said, 'None of your business.'

And he said, 'If you ever want to make it my business, just say so.'

And she said, 'Boy, I don't invest in small businesses.'

Everyone laughed. Except Dodie. And me.

There were a couple reasons I didn't laugh. The first was that I had no idea what *invest* meant. Bria's daddy wore blue suits and shiny shoes, so it made sense that she would use words like that. *Invest.* But not me. And the second reason I didn't laugh was because I didn't know whether or not I was a small business owner. I mean, I had never really seen nobody else's business at that point. And because I didn't find what Bria said funny, Dodie knew – or at least he figured – I wasn't a bully. Or a follower. Because it would've been much easier to just laugh with everybody else.

The other thing that glued me and Dodie together was that his grandmother was Mrs Monihan. *Is* Mrs Monihan. Of course, I didn't know this when we first met, but I found out when she asked me about him one night when I was hanging out at the bingo hall, chomping down fries.

'Neon, come here,' Mrs Monihan said, beckoning me how she always did, with one finger in the air. I tossed a fry in my mouth and made my way over to her. 'You know this boy?' She held up a wallet-sized photo of Dodie. 'He's new to your school.'

I ain't have to look long. Dodie was easy to recognise. 'Yes, ma'am. I know him.'

And then she did exactly what grandmothers do: told her grandson's business.

'Well, he's my grandchild. I love him, but I swear, he a downright fool. Boy got kicked out of his last school for stealing his teacher's sunglasses. And you know how they caught him?'

I almost choked.

'How?' I asked.

'Because he *wore* them to *school* the *next day*.' Mrs Monihan knocked on the side of her head. 'Anyway, if he acts up, you let me know, hear?'

'Yes, ma'am,' I said, before returning to the half-eaten cardboard canoe of crinkle-cuts waiting for me along with the confirmation that Bria Crestlake was right. Dodie was a liar. And, apparently, a thief. At least when it came to sunglasses.

But despite Mrs Monihan's request, I never snitched on Dodie. Not once in all these years. And that fool been acting up since I've known him. Been talking wild and beating his chest like he some kind of Casanova. Like he invented lovemaking and everything that goes with it.

Apparently, nobody knew nothing about kissing until Dodie came along.

Apparently, nobody knew nothing about touching until Dodie discovered oranges in the cafeteria and decided to let us know how to caress a breast, even though I told him he looked like he was in the grocery store, feeling for freshness.

'I *am*,' he said, squeezing, squeezing, squeezing.

The same way his grandmother believed she was the high priestess of bingo, that she was born lucky, Dodie acted the same way. Only difference was, Mrs Monihan actually *won* occasionally. I still don't know if Dodie knows anything about sex. If he's ever even had it. But he loves to talk about it, and he especially loves to sing about it. *Scream* about it.

Especially, especially in the car on our way to school.

'One more time, from the top!' Dodie said, turning the radio back on and starting his new song over again. Correction: his new *love* song. And before the second verse, he started pounding his pelvis against the steering wheel.

Let me explain. It's Dodie's dance move. His only dance move. If there's any kind of music, and especially if there's music he's singing, he's doing this move, which is just a series of humps and body rolls typically seen from R & B singers. But he makes it punk.

'Come on, bro. Not this. Not now,' I groaned, trying the window again. Still locked.

Dodie ignored me and went on humping the wheel, not knowing the light had turned green until the truck behind us hit the horn. Dodie almost died. And so did I since his dumb ass was mid-thrust, and he mashed the gas and brake at the same time, sending the car into convulsions, jerking into the middle of the intersection, bucking with stop-and-go.

Dodie tried to play it off, calling me a late bloomer, talking about this was what an orgasm felt like. But I knew what an orgasm felt like. Because I got hands. And it ain't feel like that at all.

• • • •

What's the opposite of punk music? What's the opposite of screams and raging guitar and thunder drums? A flute? A single violin? Whatever the sleepiest music is, that's the soundtrack of school. At least for me. Except for the beginning of the day before the homeroom bell rings, and lunch. The rest of it's a nap waiting to happen. Torture by boredom.

The beginning of the school day is always good because of Aria. She always weaves through the overflow of hormones and hecklers and hilarious nobodies pretending to be somebodies catching up on homework, which means copying homework, and complaining about class before class even starts, which I totally understand. It's like a vomit of sneakers and wrinkled T-shirts, the few kids who strangely dress like they're headed to job interviews, and kids like Dorian Blankenship, a pretty boy who, without a doubt, is going to win *Best Dressed* thanks to his older brother who made it to the NFL.

And as far as I'm concerned, the title for *Most Beautiful Girl in the School and It's Not Close* should go to the one who always sidles up to me after navigating these turbulent adolescent waters every morning to steal a hug and sneak a kiss before the day gets going.

'Good morning,' Aria said, pecking my cheek.

'Good morning.' I examined her face. Her eyes were a little off. 'You good?'

'I will be.' Aria looked up, but not at me. Past me. Up at the ceiling like she does when she's trying to keep the tears in.

'What's wrong?'

'What's wrong. . . .' She *hmph*'d. 'The real question is: *Who's* wrong? My dad had a doctor's appointment, so my mother dropped me off this morning. And I made the mistake of checking my makeup in front of her.'

'Uh-oh.' I already knew where this was going.

'So she rips into me. Again. About how my looks won't be enough. Gives me the whole speech about how skill is the only separator, and separation is the only chance at safety. And how I gotta get my act together and make a decision about what I want to do with my life.' Aria thumbed tears away, her voice a busted speaker. 'I got straight As. Scholarships to almost every college I applied to. But because I don't know what I want to study, what I want to be, she thinks I'm doomed.'

'*Doomed* is a bit . . . dramatic.' I meant it as a joke. Aria didn't take it as one.

'No, *doomed* is the actual word she used. She said, "Aria, you're doomed."'

'Damn.'

'Right.'

'But you know where it comes from.' I tried to offer some perspective.

'I do, I do. But it still ain't fair.'

The strain between Aria and her mom has been going on for the two years we've been together, but according to Aria, it's been a forever thing. The story goes that Mrs Wright, back when she was just Little Connie, was born into a tough situation and grew up in foster care until she was adopted by one of her aunts. That aunt was a jazz singer, and because she had no one to look after Little Connie, she started taking her to gigs with her. Little Connie would sit off to the side of the stage and watch the musicians play. That's when she fell for the trumpet. She wanted to learn it.

So she asked her aunt if she could take lessons, and instead of hiring a teacher, which Little Connie's aunt couldn't afford, or checking with the school, she asked her horn player, a man whose name I don't know, to teach Little Connie. And he did. He taught her to play. And he taught her other things too. Taught her to be scared. Taught her what it meant to be unsafe. Taught her that her body was also an instrument he knew how to play. Taught her how to mute her horn. How to pack it up in a box. How to carry it no matter how heavy it might have been for a girl her age.

So Little Connie, broken and afraid, began to pour everything she had into the trumpet. Barely even went to school. Just practiced and practiced until her lip calloused, which she was happy about, hoping it made her less pretty. Less desirable. She practised and practised until she was better than everyone. And by high school, she'd already become an alternate in a professional orchestra. By the time she graduated, she was one of the best.

Little Connie found her thing, and played herself to safety.

Two of the other three Wrights – Maestro and Turtle –

found their thing early too. Music. Honestly, I kinda feel the same way, because I have film. But Aria is a scholar. She's interested in learning everything there is to know just because it's there to be known. And what she'll do with a brain full of information is the one thing she just doesn't know yet.

'I just don't understand why she can't see that I've done *everything* right but be the right kind of Wright.'

'Yeah, but you're the right kind of Aria,' I said, gently pressing my forehead to hers.

'You always say that.' Her voice fanned.

'I always mean it.'

There's a thing that happens to me whenever anyone I care about cries. I cry too. I don't know why, but it's been happening ever since I was a kid. I remember one time Nat was crying because some boy lied on her. She was still in high school, and I guess he started a rumour about how she got down or whatever. And she came home and cried all night. I had no clue what had happened, or who the boy was, and the only reason I knew anything was because I kept finding reasons to walk past her room – needed to get juice from the kitchen, needed to see if Dodie was outside, needed to check on Gammy – to sneak-listen to my mother consoling her. And there was just something about hearing Nat sniffle, even though I couldn't even see the tears, that caused my own to come. So I sat outside her bedroom door and cried with her. In secret. It was pathetic, but Nat, who caught me because of all the sniffling, thought it was cute.

Fortunately, despite how embarrassing it is to do it at this age, Aria thinks it's sweet too. She did the *aww* thing she knows I hate and used one of her pinkies to dab the corners of my eyes.

'Pinky,' she said, holding it up. I ran my pinky across her cheek, clearing some of the wet.

'Pinky,' I replied, holding mine up too. We curled them around each other's. Linked them. Locked them. Like a bet or a promise or just a touch. Then Aria wrapped her arms around me and squeezed, but released just before Ms Jenkins came around the corner.

Ms Jenkins is one of those people who occasionally pops her head into the stairwells, checks that every maintenance door is locked, does bathroom sweeps, and even scopes out the hollowed space beneath the bleachers at games to make sure students aren't 'defiling the school.' She's caught me and Aria hugging too tightly for too long before, and we've had to sit through her lecture about animal instinct and detention, to which we always reply with a joke about her not wanting to see Black people hold each other.

But none of that today.

No, today Ms Jenkins walked right by me and Aria and screamed to the entire hallway, 'The bell rings in one minute! If you are not in your homerooms in one minute, you are late! If you are late, you can't learn properly! And if you can't learn properly, you can't live properly!'

I made it to homeroom on time. And guess what? Still couldn't learn properly.

First period, trig. Might as well be called *try . . . to understand*. Thankfully, no homework.

Second period, US government. Might as well be called *vote*. Only a little homework. I'd get it done in the afternoon. In biology class.

Third period, lit. Might as well be called . . . *not lit.* Or *trig*. Homework. Always.

Fourth period, lunch. Finally.

Despite the lunchroom being the typical sticky-floor conveyor belt of greasy food and things that resemble greasy food, it also, for me and my friends, doubles as a place to huddle. A meeting of the minds. Especially around the subject of yearbook work.

There are six of us.

Fred Creeks. A middle child. A movie nerd like me. And also a *nerd* nerd. He has a curious cluster of moles in the middle of his forehead that he swears is mathematically perfect. He also swears it's where angels kissed him when he was born. Because that's what his parents told him. His folks are preachers and are basically like the thirteenth and fourteenth disciples, which is funny because Fred is the only dude in our crew who I know is actually having sex. A lot of it. He and his girlfriend, Saskia, who went to a church school, are always praying and repenting about it afterward, asking for forgiveness for their sins, even though the repenting never seems to stop them from committing the sin as often as possible. His meal: pepperoni pizza and curly fries.

Tuna Randolph. Her real name is Petunia, and she's probably the coolest person I know outside of Aria and Nat. She's an artist, a painter. Got her own vibe. Keeps her hair cut low, except for a rat tail that ain't really a rat tail because it's not hanging from the back of her neck, but instead from the side of her head. She usually keeps it tucked behind her left ear. She also wears whatever she wants: paint-spotted overalls and dirty Chucks, sack dresses and Jordans. Moves how she wants. Pretty much does what she wants (hence the rat tail). And dates some of the baddest girls in the school. Her meal: nuggets and Cheetos.

Savion Gunther. The only athlete in the crew. He's on the wrestling team, which is how we got cool. (I wrestled my sophomore year. *Only* my sophomore year.) He wrestles 145 pounds and pays no attention to the strange following of girls who show up to his matches, I think for reasons that have more to do with the singlet all the wrestlers have to wear than Savion's actual skill. He's had his nose broken a few times, and there's a nose-knuckle to prove it. But he's good. *Good* good. And probably the reason I ain't have no bullies after my freshman year. None of us did. He's also the bookworm of the crew. The dude loves poetry. His meal: salad. No dressing. And an empty bottle that used to have water in it and that he was now refilling . . . with his spit.

Dodie. Sunglasses on. His meal: a cheeseburger, of course. But with Savion's salad dressing on it.

And Aria. Who's the best. Her meal . . . take a wild guess.

'I just saw your little brother in the hallway, Fred,' Aria said, sitting down. The chicken tenders on her tray were skinny, like fingers, and if I didn't know her, I might've mistaken them for mozzarella sticks. 'He looked . . . stressed.'

'Stressed?' Fred was picking a few pepperonis off his pizza. Ate them like pork cookies.

'Yeah, he was at the fountain, splashing water on his face. I asked him if he was okay, and he just nodded,' Aria explained.

'Poor kid. I'll check on him.' Fred grimaced. 'You know, he's in the tenth grade now. And y'all remember health class in the tenth grade, right?'

I knew immediately what Fred was referring to, and I

could tell by Aria's face that she wasn't catching it. But Tuna looked up from her drawing. And Savion froze his fork before stuffing another bunch of lettuce into his mouth. And Dodie, a hunk of burger between his jaws, stopped chewing. As a matter of fact, he grabbed a napkin and spit the bite into it.

And almost in unison, all of us but Aria said:

'The birthing video.'

The birthing video. It was like a rite of passage at Northlake High. It didn't matter that Ms Rambleton always told students when it was coming; there was just no way to prepare for it. No way to be ready. And years later, just the memory of it sent a collective shiver down our spines.

'Oh. I think childbirth is beautiful,' Aria said matter-of-factly.

'It definitely is. But in a ugly kind of way,' Tuna grumped, popping a Cheeto in her mouth.

We went on about health class for a few more minutes, which was really us talking about how other than the birthing video, all we remembered was how we had to repeat the words *penis* and *vagina* over and over again, as if us pronouncing the words properly would help us use the body parts they're describing.

'It might as well have been English class,' Savion joked.

'Please. *Penis* and *vagina* are way easier to understand than what Mr Gowan just assigned, even though I'm sure you'll love it,' I griped to Savion. '*The Canterbury Tales*.'

'Emphasis on *can't*,' Dodie joked.

'Emphasis on *bury*,' I countered.

'Emphasis on *yearbook*.' Aria trumped us both, refocusing the group. From there, we filled each other in on where we were with our yearbook work. Each of us had a separate assignment. I gave my video update. Status: I'd gotten 203 videos over the last seven months and only had thirty-nine to go, including mine and Aria's and the rest of Dodie's. Dodie was working on the music for the site because it was the only thing we knew he'd actually do. Savion was doing the writing and had come up with a list of random captions using quotes from poems. *Blind loving wrestling touch* to introduce the wrestling section. And *Go home and write / a page tonight* to introduce the creative writing club. And *I knew the horse meant knight* for the chess club. (It should be noted that Dodie would always tease Savion about this and say that Aria should award him the superlative *Most Likely to Graduate a Virgin*. To which Savion would respond, *I don't see nothing wrong with me being a virgin. Do you?* And Dodie would shut up before he got body-slammed.) Fred was working on the site's layout. Coding and all that was his bag. He told us he was creating a drop-down menu where each grade could be selected individually. Aria was, of course, coming up with Senior Superlatives, which, of course, I was helping her with. And Tuna was doing all the artwork. At least, she was supposed to be.

'Tuna, what you working on?' I asked. She held up her sketchbook. It was of a naked woman, but not like a naked woman just to be a naked woman, but the kind of naked that comes from modelling for artists. But there wasn't no models around.

'That's gorgeous,' Aria said. 'But I don't know if Sanchez will let us use it for the yearbook.'

'Sure we can.' Dodie chomped at the bit. He lowered

his shades and peered over the top of them. 'I mean . . . I think . . . who is that?'

'It don't matter,' Savion said. 'She ain't *Lana*.' Lana don't go to school with us either. I know her from the neighbourhood, but the rest of them know her from Dodie constantly talking about her. About how she looks better than every girl in our school, whatever, whatever, whatever.

Dodie sucked his teeth, pushed his glasses back up. 'Me and Lana just getting going. It's still new. Nothing serious yet. So, Tuna . . . who is *this*?'

Tuna glared at Dodie, bothered, which was her usual look whenever she put eyes on him. Either that or confused, like he was the most abstract piece of art she'd ever seen.

'She is exactly what she'd be to you. A figment of my imagination.'

'You right. A sweet fig meant for my imagination.' Dodie kissed his fingers, and I immediately had flashbacks of him squeezing those oranges.

'Please, you wouldn't know what to do with a girl like this, Dodie. Cut it out.'

'Oh yes I—'

'Stop.' Tuna held her hand up, closed it into a fist as if trapping Dodie's voice.

'Whatever. I—'

'Aht, aht.' Now she put a finger to her mouth.

'I—'

'No,' she snapped. 'Shhh.'

The rest of us laughed at the whole exchange. It's a thing Tuna and Dodie do often, this constant back-and-forth, bickering and chipping at each other. But it's always love. Just a different brand of it. Honestly, the running joke between me, Aria, Fred, and Savion is that Tuna and Dodie will probably end up living together one day. For whatever reason.

When Aria finished her food, I stacked our trays. And before I got up to drop them in the cleaning bin, I leaned over and asked her if she was feeling any better.

'Much better,' she said. 'I had another meeting with Mr Truss.'

Mr Truss is the guidance counsellor. Nice guy. No help.

'Did he crack the code of your future?' I ran my hand

along her back, the soft cotton of her T-shirt interrupted only by her bra, like a speed bump.

'Of course not. But we had a good time talking about all the possibilities. According to him, I could be the president of the United States.' Aria dug around in her purse, pulled out a piece of candy. Popped it in her mouth.

'You'd get my vote.' I held my hand out for candy delivery. She went back in her bag.

'Yeah, but my mother probably still wouldn't be impressed,' Aria said. 'But, hey, at least I got to skip AP Psych.'

'Sike, sike, sike!' Dodie hollered, standing up. His sunglasses now at the tip of his nose.

'What?' Aria was startled and missed the joke. We both did.

'Nothing,' Savion said, holding the bottle up to his mouth before turning away from us to spit in it. 'Just that Dodie still tripping about that girl. It's a *picture*, bro. Just a sketch.'

'Literally. Art,' Fred joined.

'Right! Like I said, if this was more than a sketch, if

she was real, you wouldn't do nothing but fumble anyway, *Dodo*!' Tuna jabbed.

'You must be sniffing . . . them pencils if you believe that,' Dodie jabbed back.

'Sniff, sniff, sniff!' Tuna . . . sniffed.

'Well, give me your sketchbook, and I'll show you what I'd do.' Dodie reached across the table, but Tuna recoiled.

'I know you don't think you 'bout to mess up my work.'

'I'm not. I promise. But y'all ain't gon' keep talking about me like I ain't the best lover at this table. I mean, I'm the writer of the new hit love song, "Empty the Clip," which I will be playing for y'all as soon as school is over. Meet me at Cherry and prepare to be turned on.'

'Pass.' From Savion.

'Yeah, me too. Pass.' This from Fred.

'Pass, pass, whatever.' Dodie shooed their rejections away. 'It's already been Neon-approved.'

Savion, Fred, Tuna, and Aria whipped their heads toward me. Aria's slightly cocked. Tuna's slightly tilted.

'I don't know if—' I tried to explain that I hadn't actually *approved* anything. But Dodie barreled on.

'Pass me the sketchbook, please.'

Tuna finally handed Dodie the book, and from there it went all . . . weird. He did his best to explain foreplay. And if I hadn't already finished eating, I would've cut the rest of my lunch short. No one had asked for it. Because don't nobody want to hear Dodie talking about *no* play. Not two-play, three-play, foreplay, four-ply toilet paper, nothing. But Dodie, trying to prove a point, went on talking about how he starts at the lips.

'I start at the lips,' he said, puckering.

'Ugh.' Tuna grimaced. But Dodie went on about how he moves down to the neck.

'Then I move down to the neck.'

'No marks,' Tuna said. 'No need to broadcast romance.'

'Some girls like that,' Dodie asserted.

'Most girls don't,' Tuna replied. Dodie went on about how he moves down to the breasts.

'Then I move down to the ti— um, the breasts.' Dodie started squeezing the air. Tuna looked like she wanted to squeeze his neck.

'They're boobs, not Hacky Sacks,' Tuna said.

'What's a Hacky Sack?' Dodie asked.

Tuna tried a new example. 'What I'm saying is, they're not . . . stress balls.'

'What's a stress ball?'

Tuna looked around the table at the rest of us, waiting on a co-signer, but me, Savion, and Fred were clueless too. We were one big shrug. Aria, noticing our blank stares, just let out a sigh.

'Be gentle,' Tuna finally said, annoyed. 'All that hard squeezing ain't cool. Just be gentle. These ain't water balloons.'

'Water balloons!' Dodie's lightbulb went off. But then he thought about it, and the bulb dimmed a bit. 'But . . . I don't squeeze water balloons because they'll bust.'

'*Exactly*. And if you squeeze some girl's boobs like that, she'll bust *you* . . . dead in your face.'

Aria almost spat lemonade all over the place, but Dodie ain't care. He just kept . . . going. Down. To what he called the . . . *volvo*.

'You mean the *vul—*' Aria started but caught herself. 'You know what, never mind.'

'I learned *that* in Ms Rambleton's class,' Dodie

boasted. 'I think I was in the AP version of sex ed. Clearly.'

Clearly.

All of this happened before I got home and holed up in my room. Before I tried drowning out the barking dog with the impossible language of Chaucer, and before I tried to distract myself from Chaucer with the senior videos, and before I was interrupted by Nat, who came to remind me of the real thing I was trying not to think about.

She'd finished her phone call and come back into my room.

'My bad, Nee,' she said, hitting the space bar on my laptop, stopping the video. I felt the bed shift under her weight as she returned to her seat on the mattress's edge. I didn't budge until she snatched the book from my head. She repeated, 'How you feeling . . . about . . . *it*?'

'Like I was born for it.'

'Nee, seriously. Come on.'

'Aight, aight.' I turned my elbows into kickstands. Propped myself up. 'I'm . . . not scared, but I'm . . . I don't know.'

'Nervous?'

'Yeah. Kinda nervous.'

Nat's eyes softened. And she ain't look surprised at all. If anything, she looked . . . relieved. Because nervous, for me, was normal. Nat was used to it. Knew how to deal with it. When we were kids, she would let me sleep in her room whenever I needed to because, well, I was a little nervous about being in the dark. Not just because I couldn't see, but because the dark seemed like something in and of itself. Like it had a fur that bristled against me. And when Curtis Whitestone said he wanted to fight me because his mother spent all the rent money at the bingo hall, Nat was the one who went with me down to the park – not to defend me, but to gas me up so I could defend myself. She told me fighting was in our blood and no one in our family ever lost. And that it was a gift we had.

And then . . . I lost. And she carried me home. And iced my eye. And told me she lied, and I still don't know if she had actually lied or if she was lying about lying to make me feel better about losing like that. And even just six months ago, when we first moved Denzel Jeremy Washington into our house, and he chased me around the living room, nipping at my ankles with his glass-shard teeth, it was Nat . . . who barked back at him. Shut him right up.

'About what?' she asked now, tapping my knee.

What was I nervous about? Um, everything. I had no idea what it would be like to be inside someone else. What it would feel like. If it would hurt Aria. What if I put the condom on wrong? What if it broke, and Aria got pregnant? My dad always told us not to bring no babies home. And what would happen *after*? What if I lost it and started tripping? What if I became addicted? I heard there's nothing better. Which means there's nothing worse. What if I . . . hated it?! What if, for some reason, our bodies just didn't work together?

What was I nervous about? *Everything.*

But, for some reason, all I could say was, 'Well, first of all, what if I can't get her bra off?'

That's what I said. It *had* been bothering me since lunch. Actually, since way before that. The clasp seemed like such a contraption, complicated even through the back of her shirt.

'What?' Nat scratched her head with a single fingernail. Patted the spot afterward.

'Her bra,' I confirmed. 'What if I can't get it off?'

'What if you can't . . . get it off?' she mumbled. Then pinched her jaw, trying to squeeze her laugh.

'I'm serious!'

Nat's eyes went soft again. 'I know you are.' She inched closer. 'Listen, this is gonna sound unromantic, but it's real. Nee, she can undress herself. It's okay. As a matter of fact, it might even be kinda hot.'

I ain't think about it that way.

'Okay, that's fair. But then Dodie was talking today about foreplay and how you gotta kiss the lips, the neck, the boobs, and then you gotta go—'

At this point, Nat was back standing. She took a deep breath. 'Dodie said *what*?'

'That there's four points to foreplay, and—'

Nat put her hand up. A *halt*. 'You listening to Dodie? Oh . . . God. There are actually *a lot* more than four. And usually, boys focus on whatever's sticking out. But trust me, the fastest way to turn a girl off is to turn her into just a body. And the easiest way to turn her into a body is to only focus on the obvious. There are lots of other erogenous zones. Hot spots. *Lots*. Like fourteen of 'em. But not everybody likes everything. So—'

'Fourteen!' I interrupted her interruption. 'How am I supposed to remember all that?'

'You don't have to.' She laughed and flicked my toe. 'This ain't no test you taking. Listen, this will be a moment where y'all can work it out together. Who knows? Might find out *you* like the backs of your knees kissed.'

'Probably not.'

'You might. *She* might.' Nat shrugged. 'The point I'm trying to make – and this is the best advice I got – is, just say the things. Say it all.'

'Say what?'

'Everything.' Nat's voice, which had been steady, now rippled into a beg. 'Tell her you nervous, Nee. Because . . . I'm sure she's nervous too. It's normal. And once y'all get that out in the open, you can *relax*. And *breathe*. And maybe even *laugh*.'

'I don't know about all that,' I grunted.

'I hear you. God forbid you actually enjoy it, right?' Nat cracked. But I didn't break.

'Come on, Nat. I'm not in the mood.'

'You not? You mean to tell me this whole time I've been wasting my good breath and even better wisdom for someone who's not even in the mood?'

'You know what I mean.'

'Do I?' She cocked her head to the side and glared.

'Seriously, I'm not playing. You think everything a joke.' I looked down at my knees, a natural response to the gravity of embarrassment. Ashy.

'Okay, okay.' Nat calmed the press. 'Hey, I'm being forreal. No more jokes. I promise. At least for the rest of the night.'

'Thanks, I guess.' I glanced up at her and sneered. Nat is Nat. I know that and love her for it, even when I hate it.

'No problem,' she said all cavalier. Then added, 'Anyway, you got any other questions, or am I dismissed?' She raised an eyebrow, smug-mugged.

Of course I had other questions. More than a few. More than she knew.

'Maybe later,' I said, picking up *The Canterbury Tales*. I laid back. Opened the book. Closed it. Then opened it again.

'Right. You got work to do.'

And twenty-four days before that . . .

I was on graveyard duty, because on Saturday mornings I'm always on graveyard duty. I wouldn't have to be if Nat were ever home, but she's not. Or if my folks ain't sleep in, but Saturday mornings are when they rest, even though neither one of them is actually resting. They just . . . stay in their room, staying and . . . rooming, if you know what I mean.

So me and Gammy got out early.

Gammy dressed in a pink blouse and a darker pink skirt, put on a full face of makeup, a freshly primped wig, and her soft shoes. The walking ones. Then she hooked a leash to Denzel Jeremy Washington's collar, luring him away from my parents' door with a treat.

'Time for your walk,' Gammy always says to him.

'Time for *your* walk,' I always say to her, grabbing her jacket from the closet.

The cemetery is almost a mile from our house, and it takes about forty-five minutes to get there at Gammy's pace, given her creaky hips, especially in the brisk April air, and the heavy purse hanging from her shoulder that she refuses to leave home. Most of that time for me was spent watching the dog, making sure he didn't lasso Gammy's legs or chew on something he wasn't supposed to be chewing on, including me. And while I would be trying to stay both close and far from that tiny beast, Gammy would gab endlessly about my grandfather.

'Did I ever tell you why Grandy always liked his clothes to be just a little bit wrinkled?' Gammy asked, pausing for Denzel Jeremy Washington to cock his leg up and pee.

'Yes. A million times. But, please, tell me again,' I said.

Gammy, sensitive to sarcasm, reached over and popped my arm.

'Watch your tone,' she ordered, tugging the leash and inching on step-by-step down the block. 'You'd be lucky to have a story like this to tell one day, grandson. Lucky.'

'Sorry,' I said, kissing her cheek. The scent of rose

perfume and that crayon-y smell of blush danced in my nostrils for a moment. 'Go ahead. Tell me.'

'Tell you what?'

Like I said, Gammy's memory is slipping, which is why she runs down the same story all the time. It isn't that she keeps forgetting she's already told us; it's that she doesn't want to forget the story itself. It's the one memory she's clung to, and it's triggered by the fact that I'm always a little wrinkled too.

'About Grandy. And the wrinkles.'

'Ah. Yeah, he loved to keep his clothes just a little bit wrinkled. You know, some whiskers in his shirts, some diagonal creases 'cross his trousers. I remember the first day I met him. He was young. Maybe twenty-one, twenty-two, and he came bopping into the laundromat I used to work at back then.' She turned to me. 'You know where that old ice-cream shop is? The one up on Jefferson?'

'Of course. Me and Aria go there all the time. That was our first date. Well, part of it. They got this cookies-and—'

'We ain't talkin' 'bout no Aria, boy.' Gammy sliced right through my romantic memory. 'She all you got on your mind? *Aria, Aria, Aria*. I bet if I opened up your head right now, all the little wrinkles in your brain would spell out that girl's name.' She wiggled her finger in the air. 'A-R-I-A.'

I just laughed. I was used to Gammy going off like this. Ain't pay it no attention. Plus, the truth was, Aria *was* on my mind. I mean, she's always on my mind, but she was on my mind different that morning, because the day before she'd gotten three emails from colleges she'd applied to, telling her she got in. With money. I was happy for her. In a real way, but also in a weird way, which is that way that made me sad for myself. But happy. For her.

'Yes, I know the place,' I said, bringing both me and Gammy back to the story. 'What about it?'

'Before it was an ice-cream whatever, that place was the old laundromat I used to work at back then. I ain't do much but sit around and break dollars and occasionally wash and fold somebody's clothes. But in them days, people ain't like you touching their garments because ain't nobody want you to shrink their stuff up. Might be the only pair of trousers they got, and don't want 'em turned into shorts,' Gammy grumbled. 'Anyway, your granddaddy came in one day. I'd never seen him before. I knew just about everybody who walked through that door, and I was certain his handsome self hadn't stepped foot 'cross that threshold until the day he did. A pretty man. Skin just as dark and smooth. Sweet mouth. And had them eyelashes that be meant for girls but only boys get. Like you.'

We waited at the crosswalk on the corner of Silver Hill and Suitland Road, Gammy taking a pause in the story to catch her breath.

'Did you say something to him?' I prompted.

'Of course I did.'

'What you say?'

'I said hello.' Gammy popped her little hip out as if reliving the moment.

'That's it? That's all you said?' I was completely unimpressed by my grandmother's game.

'Baby, it was a different time.' The light changed, and we stepped gingerly off the curb, my hand positioned on the back of her arm, ready for any stumble. 'Back then a hello was all you needed. Like dropping a line in the water. Just gotta be patient and wait for the bite.'

'But what if he don't bite?'

'Then that ain't his bait. And he ain't your fish,' she professed. 'But like I said, that was forever ago. It's different now. These days girls like your sister just jump in the water and grab her a fish. Or two.'

I laughed as Gammy rolled her eyes *for* the old school and *at* the new school.

'So clearly, Grandy was your fish.'

'Yeah, but he ain't bite immediately. And honestly, after seeing him wash clothes for the first time, I almost wanted to snatch my line back. He came in there and dumped out all his filthy overalls and dingy dungarees and shirts and whatnot, everything covered in dirt and ash and who knows what else because he was apprenticing with his father at the time, learning how to make door knockers. He put everything in the washer, washed it all up, whole time not saying a thing to me, then threw everything in the dryer. I'm just sitting there watching him, and he's just sitting there pretending to read the newspaper.'

'How you know he was pretending?'

'Because after we got together, I ain't never seen that

man pick up another newspaper a day in his life. Fool was just nervous. Or maybe he wasn't sure I was his type. And once them clothes finished drying, I wasn't sure he was mine either, because he took everything out and just threw it all back in his laundry bag. Ain't fold a thing!'

'Nothing?'

'Not slack nor sleeve. Just balled it all up like trash.' Gammy sucked her teeth as if she still couldn't believe the man she would eventually fall in love with and spend damn near the rest of her life with would commit such a crime. 'It wasn't until the third time he came in and did this that I finally asked him why.'

'You asked him why?'

'No. I didn't really ask him why. I just offered him a . . . suggestion.'

'That sounds more like you.'

'I said, "You know, if you fold your clothes, they'll be pretty much ready to go when it's time to put them on." And he looked at me and said, "The funny thing about clothes is they always ready to be put on. Because they clothes, and that's what they made for."'

'Oh, he got smart with you?' This didn't surprise me. I knew how Grandy was.

'You know how he was.' We stopped for a moment to let Denzel Jeremy Washington circle a patch of grass in one of the flower beds built into the sidewalk. Gammy loved them. Thought they made spring in Paradise Hill the best time to live there. Thought these ankle-height, iron gates outlining splashes of greenery in the middle of concrete did wonders for prettying up the blocks, and perfuming them, too.

'Hmmm.' Gammy was suddenly distracted. 'Flowers don't look like they want to open up,' she said about the sad state of the flower bed. 'Been checking every day.'

'Probably confused by the weather.'

'Maybe.' Gammy nodded. 'But they'll get there. They'll get there. Things always bloom when they ready.' She examined the closed bulbs for a moment more. 'Anyway, what were we talking about?'

'Well, I wanted to know what you thought about that?'

'About what?'

'About Grandy being kinda sharp with you.'

'Ah, yes.' Gammy flashed a devilish smile. 'Honestly, I kinda liked it. But I wasn't ready to let him win the argument.'

'But it wasn't really an argument, was it? To me, sounds like you were minding that man's business.'

'No, it was an argument,' Gammy confirmed. 'At least in my head. So I say, "Well, I guess that's true, as long as you don't mind walkin' round looking like a road map." And he started laughing. Introduced himself. *Earl Wednesday.* I loved that his last name was Wednesday. Then I introduced myself. And he said, "Miss Sharletta, I happen to actually prefer wrinkles. See, if I put my clothes on perfectly ironed in the morning, I'd spend all day trying to keep 'em that way. That don't seem like a fun way to wear clothes. But if I put them on and they're already a little wrinkled, I can actually be myself in 'em. A little imperfection takes the edge off things."'

'Was he right?' I asked as Denzel Jeremy Washington finally popped a squat.

'About them clothes? Hell, no.'

'No, about imperfection taking the edge off?'

'Ah.' Gammy's eyes shone. Tears that hadn't dropped

yet turning them to glitter. 'That ain't the point. The point is, he took the bait. *Hello!*'

To this I howled. 'Gammy, it sounds to me like *you* took *his*!' Gammy handed me a plastic bag from her purse. I bent down, cleaned up the dog poop.

'That's the way it's *supposed* to sound to you. That's what it felt like to him, too!'

After about ten more minutes we'd made it to the cemetery. Like most cemeteries, it can sometimes feel like the saddest fun house ever. Every turn the same as the last. Every landmark a headstone, which means there are no landmarks at all. But Gammy goes to the cemetery all the time. Almost every day, as long as one of us can escort her, making the trek through the maze of grass and stone to Grandy's plot.

Grandy's headstone reads HERE LIES EARL WEDNESDAY, DEVOTED HUSBAND, FATHER, AND GRANDFATHER. And built into the stone, right in the face of it, is a brass door knocker. It's in the shape of a dove, the tail serving as the knocker.

I always stand back while Gammy has her moment, and despite my urge to, I've never recorded it. This time I just stood with her and was immediately transported to the funeral a couple years back, when we were all in this place saying goodbye to him. How strange that day was. How not so strange it is now. How grass has grown up through the fresh soil he's buried under. How nature always wins.

After Gammy whispered a prayer, she reached into her bag, pulled out her rose perfume, and spritzed it all over the gray stone.

Then she said, 'Knock, knock, Earl,' and instead of using the knocker, she used her palm and patted the granite. It was a different knock than the way she knocked on every door in our house. That Gammy-one-handed thump? No. For Grandy, she had a lover's knock. A knock they both used for each other. A knock I'd heard forever and also heard about forever because Gammy always talked about it on the way home from the cemetery.

It was woven into the part of the story about how she knew she would eventually fall in love with Grandy even though he was a wrinkled mess.

'We'd been dating a few weeks. And I liked him, but it was still early. Maybe two or three dates. The first one I remember because we went to the movies. Saw something with Sidney Poitier in it when he was young and fine. You know, he was the Denzel before Denzel.'

'I know, Gammy.' Because she tells me all the time. She bats her eyelashes at me and fans her face with her hand, acting like she's hot and bothered by Sidney or Denzel, or Sidney *and* Denzel.

'Young and fine,' she repeated. 'Anyway, after that we split a tuna melt and fries, which I ordered because I wanted to have a good excuse not to kiss him, and there's no better excuse than tuna breath. But this one night he came by the laundromat. It was late, and we were already closed, and I was in there sweeping and cleaning up dryer lint when there was a knock on the door.'

Gammy wiped a tear from her eye. She always cries for Grandy, especially after leaving his grave. I wiped a tear from my eye too, because of my cry-thing. We went on. She went on.

'But that knock wasn't a regular knock. He used the palm of his hand and patted the glass, softly. Later I found out it's because he never wanted to startle me. But at the time I thought it was kind of strange. When I opened the door, he presented me with a gift wrapped in tissue paper. And you know what it was?'

'Of course I do, Gammy. But tell—'

'It was a door knocker,' she barged on. 'He'd made one for me. A circle and a triangle connected by a hinge, which, when he presented it, I had no idea what to say. Or what it was. I mean, just looked like random shapes to me. Of course, now I know that's all he could make at the time. Remember, he was an apprentice and was still learning the craft. So he wasn't that good yet, but I still loved it.'

'And that was it?'

'That was it. Wasn't too long after that I found out he definitely *did* iron his boxer shorts. And that he washed his body much better than he washed his clothes.' Her grin the biggest wrinkle on her face.

Usually, when me and Gammy get home, Ma will be in the kitchen cooking breakfast, and Dad will be asleep. Forreal this time. And this Saturday morning was no different except for the fact that there was less breakfast than usual. Less eggs. Less grits. Less bacon. And Ma was fully dressed, which was also different. Usually, she makes all this happen in an old nightshirt and a bonnet. Slippers that slap with each step. But this morning she had on clothes. Jeans and a button-down. Had her hair unwrapped and was sitting in the living room, lipstick in hand.

'Hey, how was the walk?' she asked as we came in.

'A little chilly, but fine,' Gammy said, lifting Denzel Jeremy Washington and holding him against her chest. 'Told my grandson here that he'd be lucky to have a love story like mine and your daddy's.'

'Absolutely,' Ma said, now up and heading to the kitchen.

'But all he wanted to talk about was Aria,' Gammy snitched.

'That ain't true!' I protested.

'Sounds true to me,' Ma replied, now coming back, her face holding a smirk, her hands holding plates.

I took my jacket off, tossed it over the armrest of the couch, then went and washed up in the kitchen sink, Gammy's *Aria, Aria, Aria* following me every step of the way. After drying my hands on the hand towel hanging from the stove handle, I came back to the table for breakfast, when my mother, for once, took my side.

'But you better stop talking trash about that girl,' Ma said to Gammy, who was still stroking her pup's head. 'If it wasn't for Aria, you wouldn't have your little friend there.'

'I know, I know,' Gammy said. 'I'm just messin'.' She unclipped the leash and set the dog on the floor. He shook off, then took off toward his food bowl. Gammy eased out of her jacket, handed it to me to hang in the hall closet, then headed for the sink.

Denzel Jeremy Washington was the newest member of our family, but he was a transplant, an adoptee, from the Wrights. He was originally Aria's dog, a gift from her father on her fifteenth birthday. She named him Jeremy for no reason at all, and when he came to stay with us – dual custody – Gammy renamed him Denzel Jeremy Washington and made it clear that his whole name – the *Denzel*, the *Jeremy*, and the *Washington* – had to be said every single time, and that he should never be teased for his underbite because Gammy got fake teeth and has been caught, more than once, asleep on the couch with the bottom row halfway out her mouth.

Gammy returned from the sink.

'You know I love Aria,' she said, kissing me on the cheek before sitting down at the table.

'I bet. You took her dog!' I squawked.

'Wait a minute now. That's not true. I ain't *take* nothing,' Gammy corrected me.

'Well, regardless, she lost her dog.'

'No, no. She ain't *lose* him either,' Gammy corrected me again. 'She gave him to me. Her mother didn't quite understand his form of communication.'

'You mean her mother couldn't take all that barking.'

'Whatever. The point is, we *share* him,' Gammy said. This was technically true, but it wasn't a fifty-fifty split. He's more like ninety-nine percent Gammy's dog, and one percent Aria's whenever she's over here petting him, which don't last long because . . . I mean, I'm here to be petted too.

'If you say so,' I said, reaching for a plate only for my hand to be slapped away by my mother.

'That's not for you. It's Gammy's,' Ma said.

'All this?' It was a plate of small piles. A pile of eggs. A pile of bacon. A pile of grits.

'And your dad's, when he gets up. And your sister's

when she gets home, which should be any minute because you know she with . . . that boy.'

'What boy?' Gammy said, examining the food.

'The boy she's always with on Saturday mornings. Her weekend boyfriend, Spank. And you know he can't cook for nothing. Ain't got no flavour in his personality, so I know he don't have none in his kitchen.' She pointed at the food. 'There's some for him, too.'

'So, then . . .' I was confused.

'So, then, what?'

'I mean . . . what about . . . me? Like, what I'm gon' eat?' I asked, both hungry and horrified. But Ma just hit me with the busy signal.

'Boop, boop, boop, boop . . .' She mocked me. 'Spoiled to death.'

Gammy ignored us and forked the fried eggs.

'I'm not,' I said defensively. 'I'm just saying it don't make sense that you'd cook for everybody but me. I mean, did I do something—'

'Relax, boy. I ain't cook for me neither.' Ma jacketed me with her arms from behind. 'Me and you got a date.'

'A date?'

'Yep. A breakfast date. Just the two of us.' She smushed her face against mine.

'When?'

'The moment you stop whining and get up from this table.'

I stopped whining – even though I wasn't whining – quick, and a few minutes later we were headed out. As we were leaving, Nat was coming in. Right on cue. Usually, Spank would be behind her, sniffing around for food. But this Saturday morning he wasn't.

'Good morning, Natalie,' Ma said, a smidgen of *look at you* in her tone.

'Mornin',' Nat said cheerfully.

Then Ma, checking to see if anyone had come in after her, added, 'You . . . by yourself?'

'Yeah. My car's been making a funny noise, so Spank went to get some stuff to try to fix it.'

'Ah, the boy's a handyman in more ways than one. That's *nice*,' Gammy joked from the dining room.

Nat shook off the burn. She never let any of it bother

her, and sometimes would even lean into it by threatening to divulge details.

'Okay, well, breakfast is on the table,' Ma said to Nat. 'But can you please wash up first? Your grandmother don't need to smell that boy on you.'

'Ooh, judgy, judgy!' Nat said, giving me a hug. Ma was right. I could smell him on her neck. Cigarette saliva. Gross. 'Where y'all going?'

'On a date,' I replied.

'Ain't you too old for that?' Nat asked. Mother-son dates had been going on since I was a kid, but they were usually for dinner. Ma would surprise me by taking me down to my favourite restaurant, a hole-in-the-wall burger joint called Burger Joint, not too far from the cemetery. The type of place you knew was dirty, and figured all the deliciousness was because of the filth. It was a time for just the two of us. A way for her to teach me how to, well, date. How to be a gentleman. She'd even make me pay the bill, even though I was using her money to do so. So when she said we had a date, I wasn't confused by the date part, just the time of day. We almost never had breakfast dates. But, sure enough, twenty minutes later we were pulling into the parking lot of the oldest diner in town – Bonnie's.

My mother touched up her lipstick before getting out the car. Then waited for me to hold the door for her before entering the restaurant. We slid into a booth, the yellow vinyl farting with each scoot.

The waiter came over immediately and filled the plastic water cups that were positioned in front of us on the table. The kind that look like glass but ain't.

'My name is Rochelle, and I'll be your server this morning. Can I get y'all something to drink besides water? Tea? Coffee? Juice?'

'Coffee for me,' Ma said, taking a menu.

'For me too, please.'

'Cream and sugar?' Rochelle asked. My mother shook her head. I nodded.

'Got it.' Rochelle walked away, and even though my mother had the trifold menu flapped open, we both knew exactly what we were getting. Whenever we have breakfast anywhere outside the house, I always order pancakes, because even though Ma cooks pancakes at home sometimes, they never taste quite as good as pancakes outside. Other things are better inside. Like eggs. Something about eggs cooked at home makes them taste better than eggs out. Same with sausage. And definitely bacon. But pancakes? They shine when they come from a greasy griddle.

'So, Neon . . . ,' Ma interrupted my pancake pondering, and dug around in her purse. I would've thought she was looking for hand sanitiser if she hadn't called me Neon. She never calls me that. No one close to me besides Aria calls me that. It's Nee. And the only time my mother adds the *on* is when it's about to *be* on. And this was one of those times, because then she said, 'I found this in your room.'

If this were a movie, these few frames would be in slow motion as my mother pulled a gun from her purse. Or a little zip of weed. Or a paper bag full of money. But none of those things were in my room.

Instead, Ma pulled out . . . a bra.

Brown and lace.

Slapped it on the table like a winning ace.

My mouth fell open. She put her hand up to stop

whatever words may have potentially been coming, but there was no need. Because there were no words.

'Before you say anything, just know I'm not here to judge you. But I need you to tell me how one of my bras got under your bed.'

Just then the waitress returned to the table with coffee. She looked at the bra and somehow managed to set the coffee down.

'Oh . . . um . . .' Rochelle clearly wasn't sure what to say next. And who could blame her?

'Pancakes, please. A short stack for me. A full stack for him, with an order of fries.' My mother put in our order without skipping a beat.

'Are breakfast potatoes okay?' Rochelle asked, eyes flicking back to the bra.

'Nah, he prefers French fries,' Ma said.

'Coming right up.' Rochelle damn near ran to the kitchen. And my mom ran the question right back toward me.

'So . . . exactly why was one of my bras in your room, son?'

'Why were you in my room, Ma?'

‘Don’t do that. Also, me and your daddy’s names are on that deed. So your room is mine,’ she said, pursing her lips for a second. ‘Now, why—’

I cut her off because I did *not* want to hear that question in public again! ‘I don’t know.’

‘You don’t know?’ Ma seemed immediately disappointed. She forced an exhale. ‘I’ve always looked at us as having an open line of communication. We don’t lie to each other. At least, I thought we didn’t.’

I looked down. Couldn’t stomach her face.

‘Are you wearing it?’ she asked bluntly. ‘Because if you are, just say so.’

‘No!’

‘You sure? Listen, I have questions, but, like I said, no judgment. I promise.’

‘Ma. I’m not wearing it.’ Eyes still on my lap, the cause of all this.

‘Nee, look at me,’ she said. And I did. ‘So then, what’s going on?’

I glanced up to see some of the other servers stretching their necks to get a glimpse of the lacy cups on the table next to the plastic ones that looked like glass. Rochelle must've run her mouth. Again, who could blame her?

Noticing the eyes as well, my mother folded the bra up, tucked it back down into her bag.

'Neon,' she encouraged.

I took a deep breath, and if there had been a deeper breath available, I would've taken that one too. Three, two, one, exhale.

'Me and Aria . . .' That's as far as I got. Our names. But I wasn't sure where to take it next. How far.

'Yessss?'

'We . . . been talking about how our anniversary's coming up. Two years. And . . . we, um . . . we think we're ready to . . . you know?'

'I don't,' she said. But she did. And I knew she did because of her smirk.

'Ma . . .'

'Okay, okay. You and Aria are thinking about having sex.' She just laid it out, just like that. I didn't confirm or deny. I didn't have to. 'But what does that have to do with my bra?'

She took a sip of coffee.

'I wasn't sure how to, um . . . how to work them. So I just thought it might be helpful to, uh, practise. The hooks are . . . tricky.'

She choked. Almost spat coffee in my face. Tried to get it together before responding.

'Sorry,' she said, dabbing her mouth. Took a sip of water. Dabbed her mouth again. 'Yeah, yeah, I guess that's true.' Then she looked at me as if I wasn't seventeen. As if I'd shrunken right there in that booth. As if my face softened, rounded back into the dough it used to be. As if the patch of fuzz on my chin that was struggling to be a beard had retreated back into my face. As if I'd lost a tooth and the deep in my voice and had become her baby again. Little Nee Nee.

'I guess I shouldn't be surprised,' Ma said at last. 'You ain't Little Nee Nee no more.'

'You mad?' I asked.

'About you foolin' around with my bra? Yes! You got no idea how much those things cost, and you in there *hookin'* and *unhookin'* like it's some kinda toy.'

'No, I mean . . . you mad about me and Aria—'

'Wanting to have sex?'

'Yeah.'

'No.' She leaned forward, put her elbows on the table. 'I'm not upset about that. But, Nee, there *are* some things I need you to know.'

The last time my mother told me there were some things she needed me to know, I was twelve, and for whatever reason, I'd gone through a strange period where I'd refuse to take a bath. Not sure why. It's just one of those weird things boys do, I guess. I used to go in the bathroom, run the water in the tub, splash my hands in it, then drain it. Until one day my mother sat me down and said, 'There are some things I need you to know,' which was followed by 'You stink' and 'I can see the dirt around your neck.' Which was followed by her taking cotton balls and alcohol and showing me the said dirt around my neck. And a follow-up conversation not with my father, which would've been easy, but with my grandfather, which wasn't *not* easy but wasn't nice.

I was hoping this didn't go that way.

'The first thing,' Ma said, holding a finger up, 'is about

protection and consent, but we covered that a long time ago. Do you need a refresher?'

'No.'

'*Means no.*' She pointed at me, then continued. 'The next thing I need you to know is that young ladies are human beings, not sofas for you to jump around on. Is that clear?'

I nodded.

'Number three.' Three fingers in the air. 'Pay attention to her. If it looks like it hurts, it does.'

For some reason, that one embarrassed me. Maybe because of all the videos I'd seen where no one seems to be paying much attention to that at all.

'Which leads me to number four. All them movies you watch—'

'What movies?'

'Nee . . . you think I'm dumb? All those extra-long showers? With your phone?'

'Oh . . . I don't take—'

'Ain't nothing wrong with masturbating,' Ma said as Rochelle appeared with the pancakes. And now I wanted to run back to the graveyard I'd visited earlier with Gammy and make myself a new home there.

'Short . . . stack and a full stack,' Rochelle said, setting the plates in front of us, a weird smile across her face. 'And an order of fries. Anything else?'

'We're fine,' I said. And the moment Rochelle walked away, I said, 'Ma, you think you can lower your voice?'

'Oh, I'm sorry. Of course,' she whispered, but that was the only thing she whispered. After that she returned to her usual volume, which, in this case, was a few decibels too high. 'But I'm serious, ain't nothing wrong with masturbating, Nee. I just don't want you to think them movies are accurate depictions of what sex is like. They're movies. And you of all people know movies ain't real. Not to mention, Aria ain't those women. And you . . . ain't those men.'

'What you mean?'

'Son . . . I gave birth to you. You *know* what I mean.' Ma poured syrup on her pancakes. 'Also, you ever noticed in those things that they call Black men BBCs? As if all y'all are, are big black—'

'Ma, please. Don't.' I was already struggling knowing

my mother knew what I was doing, and struggling even more knowing she, apparently, had watched porn. What I didn't need in this very busy diner was for her to say what *BBC* stood for. I'd honestly rather have had Denzel Jeremy Washington turn my toes into chew toys.

'I'm not gonna say it. I'm not gonna say it,' she chanted, wagging her head. 'The point I'm trying to make is, you're a whole person. Not just a penis.' She spread butter across the top of her short stack. 'That being said, masturbation's healthy. Ain't no shame in it.'

'Healthy?' I had never heard it put that way. Ms Rambleton just had us repeat the word and definition. And then we'd all cracked jokes and pretended none of us ever did it. Of course I know now that all of us were lying.

'Sure. Get to know yourself.' She cut a fluffy triangle from her stack of pancakes, folded it into her mouth. 'Think about it. How you gon' be able to tell someone else how to please you if you can't please yourself?'

My stomach hurt. Appetite blown.

'Okay, is there anything else?' I leaned back, about to slide under the damn seat.

'Actually, yes. *Two* more things,' Ma said. *Great*, I thought. 'First, put your finger in your ear.'

'Ma.'

'Put your finger in your ear.'

'Right now?'

'Right now.'

I did as I was told. Stuck my index finger in my ear.

'Now, wiggle it around,' she said.

I wiggled it around.

'Like this?' I asked.

'A little more.'

I wiggled more.

'Now, tell me, what feels better when you do that, your finger or your ear?' Ma asked. I thought for a moment, wiggled my finger in my ear even more.

'My ear feels better.'

'Exactly. Women are meant to feel pleasure too. Understand?'

I nodded, both mortified and mystified. 'And . . . the last thing?'

'The last thing is, well, I bet you thought once this day

came, I would say something to you about not doing it. And it ain't like I'm rushing you to do it, because there's nothing wrong with waiting. But I'm not surprised you want to. So I'm not going to try to talk you out of it because I think that would be silly on my part.'

Now, *this* surprised me.

'Silly?'

'Of course. Because what I know is that anyone who has ever had an orgasm will do anything to have another,' she said with a knowing nod. 'So if y'all decide to go there, just take care of each other on *every* return visit. Got me?'

I just nodded and reached for the syrup.

The rest of breakfast and the car ride home were strangely normal. I'm not sure what I was expecting, but after Ma said all the uncomfortable stuff she needed to say and we pulled up in front of the house, she added, 'You can always talk to me about this. Or anything.' And 'I love you.'

'Love you too, but I'm not sure I want to talk about this ever again.'

Nat's not-boyfriend Spank was outside, his body half

under the hood of Nat's car as if her old beater were a metal monster in the middle of eating him alive. Which my parents would've loved.

'Before we go in, let me ask you: Have you and your dad talked about any of this?'

'Not really,' I said, recalling a moment some months back where we sorta talked about it but sorta didn't. 'Not *forreal* forreal.'

'Do you want me to tell him?' Ma asked.

'If I tell you not to, you gon' tell him anyway?'

'Yes. But you know your father. All he's gonna say is "Don't bring no babies in here unless they know how to count money."'

My dad has been saying that for as long as I can remember, mainly to my sister. When she was in high school, he'd practically preach it to her.

Don't bring no babies in here unless they can count money. I don't need no grandchild, I need an accountant to help with the bingo books.

Nat would always respond with 'But y'all were teenagers when y'all had me, and look at how I turned out!'

And then Dad would say, 'Yeah . . . look at how you turned out?' But he was always joking. The truth is, Nat can do no wrong. Not to him. Doesn't matter what she has going on; she's his baby girl, his pride and joy, and everything she knows about men, he taught her. How to listen for the lie. How to protect herself by using what he calls *the Doorknob*.

You grab and twist! he'd instruct, demonstrating the move.

'I just don't know why Nat's never given that boy the Doorknob,' Ma said, now confirming she could read my mind. We peered at Spank through the windshield.

'Maybe she has,' I said, opening the car door.

'Yeah, maybe she has,' my mom said unenthusiastically. Then, lowering her voice, she added, 'And maybe he likes that kinda thing, and that's why he can't seem to get away from her.'

The thing about Spank is that the way my folks talk about him, you'd think he was the worst person ever. You'd think he was some cliché clown with *scumbag* tattooed across his neck and whatever else parents see as inappropriate or unsavoury for their daughters to date and their sons to be. But the truth is, Spencer Hankinson, or Spank as everyone knows him, ain't none of that. He's a *regular Ronnie.* Rocked an old-man high fade, wore blue jeans that were the middle wash, not the dark or the light but that blue that looked both childish and fatherly, and white T-shirts out the pack, except for when he wore the black ones out the pack. And this time of year, a standard gray hoodie. He had a job as a bank teller, and smoked cigarettes, which might've been the one edgy thing about him if cigarettes weren't so corny. What drove everyone up the wall about him – and by everyone I mean my folks – is that he wouldn't walk away from Nat even though he was only her boyfriend/not-boyfriend on Fridays and Saturdays. The other days of the week were for . . . the other guys.

Mondays and Tuesdays, she was hanging out with Preston Creeks, Fred's older brother, so definitely a church boy, but not a church boy at all according to Nat. And Fred. Wednesdays and Thursdays was for Charlie Last-Name-Unknown. We didn't ask much about him. And she didn't talk much about him. And Fridays and Saturdays were Spank's days. The best of the bunch. The one who seemed to really care about Nat whether or not she cared about the fact that he cared. And she did. She just wasn't interested in anything more from him or any of them.

'I'm just dating,' she would say. 'What's wrong with that?'

Most days that made sense to me, but on the days when Spank would be doing things like he was doing that Saturday, trying to fix her car, I have to admit, it confused me. But I never found the courage or the moment to ask him about it.

After getting out of my mom's car, I said, 'Wassup,' but he didn't hear me, so I doubled up. 'Wassup, wassup . . . Spank.'

Spank craned his neck from behind the raised hood.

'Wassup, Nee. Hi, Mrs Benton.'

'Hi, Spank.' Ma paused, looked into the guts of the car, shook her head. 'I see she got you out here working.'

'Yes, ma'am.' Spank wiped his hands on his jeans. 'It's nothing too serious. Just fixing the timing belt.'

'Yeah, well, you know what they say. Gotta make sure the timing belt is . . . on time,' Ma said, patting him on the shoulder. She had no clue what a timing belt was. Neither did I.

I didn't go inside. My mother did, and I wanted to, but I also didn't want to because it felt weird to go in knowing my dad was there and that my mom was definitely going to tell him about our conversation, and I just wasn't ready for a family meeting about all this. So I stayed on the porch. Zipped my jacket to the top. Took a seat on the step. Pulled out my phone. Videos.

State your name.

Serena Clark.

And how would you describe high school in three words?

People are weird.

State your name.

Shuckey Mutton. I can say Shuckey, right? Or you need governments?

Nicknames are fine.

Cool.

How would you describe high school in three words?

Ball is life.

State your name.

State your name.

State your name.

State your name.

Savion Gunther.

How would you describe high school in three words?

Hmmm. I think for me it would be something like . . .

Mind your business.

Word.

Why you looking at me like that?

I just wasn't expecting that. Thought you'd say something about wrestling. Like, No holds barred or something like that.

That's a good one, but nah. It's definitely Mind your business.

State your name.

State your name.

State your—

'You good, man?' Spank asked. He was leaning against my sister's car, taking a smoke break. Because of where I was sitting, the sun was blinding me, turning him into a silhouette, a voice, and a scent. Cigarettes really do smell terrible. Even outside.

'Yeah, just looking through these videos.'

'Videos for what?'

I put my hand up to my eyebrows to block the sun.

'Nat ain't tell you? I'm on the yearbook staff at school. Me and my friends. But we making it digital. So I'm shooting short videos of the whole senior class, asking each student to describe high school in three words.'

'Three words?'

'Just three words,' I said, pressing play on Fred's video, which I'd just scrolled back to. I held the phone up so Spank could hear it.

State your name.

Fred Creeks.

How would you describe high school in three words?

A good—

I stopped the video because it hit me like a cell phone upside the head that Fred's older brother, Preston, is Nat's Monday-and-Tuesday not-boyfriend. *Yikes.*

'What happened?' Spank asked.

'Oh . . . I just—'

'Play the rest.'

I wasn't sure what was coming. Or what he would say. Or if he would say anything. Or if he even knew.

'It's cool, man,' he assured me. 'Play it.' And I knew he knew.

I did what he asked and started the video over.

State your name.

Fred Creeks.

How would you describe high school in three words?

A good time.

A good time? That's it?

A blessed *time.*

Spank listened closely and puffed his cig. 'I like that, I like that.' He nodded. That's all. He ain't say nothing about Preston, and seemed completely unconcerned. 'What about yours?' he asked.

'I ain't do mine yet. Haven't found my three words.' I put my phone to sleep. 'What you think yours would've been?'

Spank put the cigarette out on the bottom of his sneaker, then slid the half smoke back in the box of wholes.

'Oh, I know *exactly* what mine would've been,' he said,

turning back toward the car. He peered down into the belly of it. Or maybe it was the brain. He grabbed his wrench and went on wrenching whatever he'd been wrenching. 'Mine would've been about your sister. Something like *Nat don't care.*'

'Nat don't care?'

'Nat don't care. Because back then she *didn't* care. She wasn't checking for me at all in high school,' he said, turning toward me. His face was all goofy. 'You gotta remember, I've known Nat since ninth grade, and had a crush on her from day one. But I wasn't . . . her type.'

'What was her type back then?' I asked, not really sure if my sister got much of a type now.

'Not me.' Spank shrugged. And tugged. 'That's all I know. But it's cool now.'

'I guess,' I murmured, returning to the videos. I played Fred's again. Laughed at the way he said *blessed* like he was on the pulpit. Like he was preaching. Then I skipped to Tuna's.

Everything works out.

I wasn't expecting that from Tuna, but when I looked

at the video, at her face, I remembered what was going on with her. I'd recorded her a few months back, and at that point it had been a few months since she'd spoken to her father. Or a better way to say it is, it had been a few months since he'd spoken to her. Which was wild because he was her best friend. Taught her how to draw and paint. Taught her how to dress too. They were close like me and Nat. So much so that when Tuna came to the realisation that she liked girls, she wanted her father to be the first to know. Only problem was, he didn't want to know. Or believe. Or accept. Or even . . . talk.

Everything works out? I say on the recording.

I hope so, Tuna says.

'It does,' Spank testified from under the hood. He'd still been listening. 'Not always how you expect it to, but it does. That's for sure.' Then he said, 'Come hold this.'

I slipped my phone in my pocket and came over to the car, held the wrench he'd been using in place while he dug down and tried to connect a piece of elastic that I guess was the timing belt to whatever it was supposed to be connected to.

'Okay, so how did it work out between you and my sister? This the way you imagined it?'

Spank wiped sweat from his forehead, oil streaking across it like painted-on wrinkles.

'That's a good question,' he said, but he didn't answer it. At least, not immediately. Instead, he asked a question of his own. 'You know why I like Nat?'

Because you a duck? Because you ain't got no game? Because you insecure? I was thinking all kinds of stuff but wouldn't say a word. Just waited for him to answer it himself, hoping I would finally have a clue.

'Because she's a good friend. We're good friends. I mean, yes, we're more than friends, but that don't mean we *belong* to each other. I don't own her. She don't own me. And the only thing we owe each other is respect. Because . . . that's what friends do.'

'That's what weirdos do,' I said, half joking.

'It's just called *dating*,' he said, echoing what Nat always says. 'And if me and Nat ever agree to make it more, we will.'

'That's just because y'all old. For my generation, there's

talking to, messing with, dealing with, and being with,' I explained.

'Okay, okay.' Spank grabbed the wrench from me. 'And which of these is you and Aria?'

'We in the *being with* category. Obviously.' I said it with some bass.

'Fair enough.' Spank nodded. 'But what about when y'all graduate? Last night Nat told me about the door knocker you asked her to make for Aria.'

'Yeah. I mean, I was just waiting for her to get accepted somewhere. And yesterday she got the first yeses, so . . .'

'So . . . what happens when she leaves?'

To that I had no answer, so I added all this to the list of things I wanted to talk to Aria about. Also on that list was (1) did she have bait? And did it work on me? And (2) my mother taking me on a breakfast date to talk about sex. And now I was adding a third: (3) does she believe in *dating*? More importantly, was she planning to *date* when she went away to school? But I wasn't sure if I'd actually ask that part. Because we promised each other when she started applying that we wouldn't talk about it until we had to. Plus, she'd just started getting her acceptance emails, and it didn't seem right to make her moment all about me. We were still celebrating. Even though I was curious.

And by curious, I mean nervous.

And by nervous, I mean . . . kinda worried, just because deep down, I knew Aria loved to know things, so why wouldn't she want to know other people? And I agreed with Spank that Aria was my friend first – she really, really was – but if I was being honest, I just didn't know how I'd feel. And what about when she came home for summer break? Was I going to be like Spank? Coming over to fix her car? I don't even know how to fix cars! But if I could, would I? I mean, I did help her paint her house before she ever even went out with me, so . . . I guess I would. But what did that mean? Was I shaping up to be her summertime link? Her hidden hometown hookup? Was I tripping? Yes. I was tripping. I know Aria, and she knows me. And we know . . . what we know. And that's enough. Maybe. Definitely tripping. Which is why we don't talk about it. Not to mention, there's still months and so many movies to watch before she goes, so many other things to be concerned about, like what ice cream we'll get after a film. Because that's our thing: movies, then ice cream. On Sundays.

For movies, King Cinema is our place. It's an old theatre that only shows ancient films. Flicks from the sixties. Seventies. The reason we do it on Sundays is because I don't have to work at the bingo hall, and the theatre's only a few blocks from the church my mother makes our family go to every week. Not because we're religious – Gammy is – but because it's the one thing Ma, Dad, Gammy, Nat, and me do together. My added incentive is the after-church date where I get to watch a movie with my girl. In dress clothes. Which she always likes. Says I look good like that. I always correct her and say I look gooder than she don't know what. She always agrees.

We always get there early enough to catch the previews, which are also old, and to have time to talk before the lights go out, which is important because there's no talking when the movie starts.

We use that pre-movie time to chat about almost

everything. A list from the day before. Family stuff. Career goals. Our wild friends. Bingo-hall characters. The yearbook. A few months back we even chose our date to connect, to be together, sitting right there in those dusty burgundy seats. Or at least, an estimated date.

'Are you sure you want to? Because I'm sure,' Aria said.

'You sure, you sure?' I'd asked, to make sure.

'I think so.'

'So, you *think* you sure?'

'No, I know. I'm sure. But . . . when?'

'I'm not rushing you. Or this. But . . . how about right now?' I leaned in for a kiss. That was a joke, and thankfully, Aria laughed, mid-smooch, my lips grazing her teeth. And *thankfully* thankfully, she didn't say okay, because I was *not* ready, despite what I was feeling.

Before saying anything else, Aria thought for a second. Thought and thought and thought. And then.

'Okay, so it's January now. Maybe we . . . plan for sometime around our second anniversary.' Now she sounded even more sure.

'So . . . May?'

'Yeah.' She smiled. 'Spring seems right.'

I nodded, happy the lights were dimming but scared my grin would show brighter. I turned away until the screen came on. Previews.

Then the feature presentation.

The best part is she always sneaks fries in for me.

The best best part is when she acts like she's laying her head on my shoulder, but she's really just trying to kiss on me.

The best best best part is when she lets me put my hand down her shirt.

The best best best best part is when she runs her hand up my leg.

And the worst part, every week, is when Mr and Mrs Stanfield come in. An old couple who always sits right next to us. It don't matter where we're sitting; they always come and take the seats beside us. They think we're a film club, but we're not.

We're boyfriend and girlfriend, looking for a dark room to work everything out in. A place to have a blessed time.

And twenty-four weeks before that . . .

It was Halloween weekend. And instead of doing something romantic and corny with Aria, like pumpkin carving or whatever, I was with my dad after school, helping him prepare for the Friday rush down at the bingo hall. This meant we were taking inventory of food (Are there enough chicken tenders and fries? Who's making the potato salad?!); making sure all the kitchen equipment – which was only a griddle and a deep fryer – was prepped (Is the oil fresh?); making sure we received the drink order, including pallets of canned sodas, a few cases of wine, and two kegs of beer; and lastly, running to the bank to make sure we had enough cash to pay the winners. My father does all this every day by himself, but on Fridays, which are usually paydays for most people, I come in early to help him out with it, just because we're guaranteed to be busy. These be the days the hall goes from a cool, casual experience, damn near sleepy – with Dad calling out numbers to the regulars, all relaxed and calmly stamping their sheets and small-talking with their neighbours and gambling buddies – to Fridays with the players who come to pretend they're in Vegas. Like they got enough money to let fly. Loud and all over the place like they ain't never been nowhere. Add Halloween to the mix and . . . *boom*.

'I'll try to get your mother to walk him tomorrow morning for Gammy,' Dad said as we came into the kitchen of the hall. He was talking about the new dog, who had been barking nonstop, like he'd never been nowhere. And when it came to pooping, he'd been . . . everywhere. All over the place. It had been his first night with us, and it was clear he wasn't used to our house. Hadn't been trained for it. And we hadn't been trained for him. So that morning we woke up to turds peppering the floor of his crate. Some still whole, others smashed and smeared.

Dad complained about it in the car, all the way from our house to the bank and from the bank to the hall.

'Nat would do it, but she ain't gon' be home. And I know you scared of dogs—'

Dad had tucked the pouch of money in the safe, and now we were restocking the drinks.

'Not scared,' I retorted. 'I just don't like them, especially the ones I know don't like me.'

'Right. You don't like them. But I need you to at least try to help out until we get him on his do-his-business routine. Y'all might even get used to each other. Plus, Gammy can take him with her when she goes to the graveyard to visit Grandy. That way she can walk him with some supervision,' Dad said. 'But something's gotta give, because in addition to the poop—'

'And pee,' I added. Wouldn't want him to forget that detail.

'And pee, his little ass barked all morning. All morning, Nee. Barked and barked and barked while I was trying to sleep.'

'At least he wasn't trying to bite your feet,' I said, talking about how I had to sit on the couch with my legs tucked under me this morning as me and Gammy watched the beginning of *Mississippi Masala*, of course. Before Dodie came to get me. Then, realising this wasn't about me, added, 'But yeah, he's a barker.'

'Well, I'm a worker who also needs to be a sleeper. So we gotta figure this out.' Dad pointed to a stack of boxes behind the bar. My task, assigned. 'What I will say is, I ain't heard your grandma laugh that hard in two years. As much as I loved your grandfather, I realise now that what I loved most about him was how happy he made Gammy. She's different with that dog. It ain't even been twenty-four hours, and she already got a little light back in her.'

Dad started ripping plastic from the pallets of soda cans so he could load the fridge. After five cans, he yawned. After another few, he yawned again.

'You sure you don't need me to call the numbers tonight?' I asked, opening the box of red wines. To call the numbers was the best job at the bingo hall. At least to me. I grew up watching my father turn the spherical steel cage full of wooden balls, each with a letter and number painted on it. B23. O17. N98. He'd sit up on a platform with the cage and a microphone, and announce each ball that dropped from it, everyone waiting for the right combination of numbers to match the ones on their cards so they could yell bingo. He was basically the announcer of luck. And I liked that, and wanted to do it.

'Absolutely not,' he said to my offer. 'You'll have your chance one day, but not today. Today you gon' do *your* job, which is . . .'

'Payouts. I know.'

'Hey, at least you get tips! I'm the one who's actually turning the numbers, so really I should get the tips. But noooo, pay the *adorable teenage boy* just for being able to count.' He reached over and tried to pinch my cheek, but I dodged him.

'Chill.'

'Oh, you too old for me to pinch your cheeks?'

'Yeah. I am,' I said, flat. Dad laughed.

'Okay, well, are you too old to put on a costume tonight?'

What he was talking about was that tonight was Neon Bingo's Annual Halloween Night, which just meant everyone who worked at the hall, or came to play, had to be dressed in a costume. My father's Bigfoot costume he wore every Halloween was in his office closet, where it lives all year until this night, which is when he breaks it out, sprays it down with air freshener, and throws it on. Again. Then he struts out onto the bingo floor like it's the first time people have seen it. Or . . . smelled it.

I, on the other hand, have worn all kinds of costumes over the years, from monsters, to clowns, to superheroes, to cartoon characters. But this year I felt different. Older. And didn't want to do the whole dress-up thing. Plus, I was planning to leave early. I was supposed to be meeting up with Aria, Fred, Dodie, Savion, and Tuna to talk about how to approach our roles as the newest yearbook staff. Mr Sanchez had just accepted our proposal to change the format of the yearbook, from a book to a website. It was Aria's idea. She realised, after we'd taken our senior photos at the beginning of the school year, that there would be no documentation of our final days of high school. No pictures of our class trip. No prom pictures. No graduation pictures. Because the book has to be turned in early enough to be printed and delivered before the end of the year. So to fix that problem, Aria suggested we put it all online. That way we can document up to the last minute.

She's brilliant like that.

So, because I had a meeting to go to, to talk about a serious matter, which of course would morph into some unserious shenanigans, I decided that instead of putting on a whole costume, I'd just wear a rubber mask Aria got me, a gag gift for my last birthday. Of Spike Lee's face.

'I'm putting on a costume,' I responded to my father's question. 'Just not a *whole* one like you. A mask is still a mask. It counts.' Dad just nodded and started lining up the Sprites. 'Plus, you said I can leave early for the yearbook thing.'

'Right.' He flashed a look. 'The yearbook thing.'

'I told you about it.'

'I know you did.'

'So why you acting like I didn't?'

'I'm not. I'm acting like I know teenage boys.'

'Which means what?' I didn't know it was happening, but my voice had sharpened.

'Relax, Nee. I'm not on your back about nothing,' he said, grabbing more soda cans. 'I just know when I was young, I would've joined anything and done anything to be around my girl too.'

'Everything ain't about Aria. I really like . . . yearbooks.' I took the last bottle of red from the box. Cabernet.

'Cool.' My father looked at me. Chewed his jaw to keep from chuckling. 'Maybe I was just . . . different when I was your age.'

'Different how?' I was so annoyed.

'Listen, when I was seventeen I was trying to be everywhere your mother was. If Brina went, I went. If Brina didn't want to go, I didn't want to go either. She could've asked me to join the math club, and I would've been in there adding and subtracting like it was my whole purpose in life.'

'That's not really how me and Aria are.'

He nodded, but it was one of those gestures that was meant to be read as opposite. He was nodding and saying he got me, but he ain't get me. Not at all. And I could tell because he just stared at me as if my face had become a word search.

'What?' I asked.

'Nothing,' he said, curling his hand, beckoning for me to pass him the empty box the wine bottles had come out of.

'Dad, what?' I cocked my head. 'Why you keep looking at me like that?'

'I'm not looking at you like nothing.' He broke the box down, tossed it in the corner for me to take out later.

'Yes, you are.'

'Okay, so then what am I looking at you like, Nee?'

'I don't know. Like you got something to say.'

'But I don't have nothing to say.' He went and grabbed the fresh oil for the deep fryer. Set it on the steel counter. 'Actually, there *is* something I want to say.' He cracked and spun the top off, peeled the aluminum seal from the mouth of the gallon jug, then began to pour the oil into the fryer, the slow glugs a metronome for the awkwardness. 'Really, something I want to ask. I mean, I don't want to ask, but as a father, I feel like I need to.'

I had already opened another box of wine. The whites.

'Go for it,' I said.

'You and Aria, y'all been together for a while now, right?'

'Yep. About a year and a half.' Confusion. 'That's what you wanted to ask?'

'Nah,' he said, squaring up. 'You still a virgin.' He just said it. Didn't ask, just said. As if it were a fact.

'Yeah, I'm still a virgin. So what?' I shrugged.

'Good for you.' No sauce on it. No season. Just dry and healthy.

'Don't feel like it. I mean, if it's so good for me, then why you bringing it up like this?' I asked, lining up the Chardonnays in the bar fridge. To say I had thought about having sex with Aria once or twice would have been the worst lie ever told. To say I'd thought about having sex with Aria at least once every hour . . . would still have been the worst lie ever told. I thought about it more than I'd like to admit. And more times a day than I could count.

'Just . . . wondering. But ain't no shame in being a virgin, kid,' Dad said. 'I just figured – I mean, just looking at y'all yesterday . . . the way you held her hand.'

Dad rarely sees Aria. He rarely sees me around her. But yesterday afternoon, before he headed down to work, Aria showed up. With her dog, Jeremy. She had tears in her eyes, and her father and little sister flanked her for support.

This moment had been in the works for almost a week. It started with a shaky-voiced phone conversation, Aria telling me her mother was fed up with the barking. Telling me her mother couldn't tell the difference between her trumpet and the dog, and she needed to be able to do so because she was world-famous. Telling me her mother also said her little sister, Turtle, couldn't concentrate on her singing with all that yapping, and that voice was a more important investment than Aria's snuggles. So unless Aria was deciding on the spot to focus on, maybe, being a veterinarian, it was time for the dog to go.

'Go where?' I asked. 'You taking him back to the shelter?'

'I asked my mother if that's what she wanted me to do, and she got even madder at me,' Aria explained. '"Why would you suggest a shelter, Aria? The damn dog barks too much, but it doesn't deserve to be in prison!" She went on and on, and was so upset, she looked like she was going to cry. And then she stormed back to her practice room. Slammed the door.'

'Oh, wow. Okay, so, a shelter's not an option.'

'But she didn't give me any better ones,' Aria said. 'Poor little guy only barks because he has a nervous condition from previous trauma!' Her voice now became furious.

'I know,' I said.

'I think my mother just hates me,' she said.

'She doesn't,' I said. 'She loves you. She just has—' I caught myself about to say the most cliché movie line of all time. So to avoid that, I said, 'Stuff. She just has . . . stuff. We all do.'

'Yeah, I guess.'

'So what's the plan?' I asked.

'I just want to make sure I can see him sometimes, and that he's somewhere safe and loving.' Pause. 'You think . . .' Pause. 'Maybe he can . . .' Pause. 'Live with . . .' Pause. 'You?'

'No.' Not even a little pause.

'Damn, Neon. Thanks for supporting me in my time of need.'

'I'm not trying to be mean. It's just – you know that dog don't like me. Plus, you know I'm kinda . . . nervous around him.'

'Yeah, but for no reason.'

'For no reason? He don't rock with me, Aria! Be trying to bite me every time he sees me.'

'He's playing—'

'He's also growling.'

'He's joking—'

'And barking.'

'See, you just like my mother.'

'You don't mean that.'

'I don't. But still.'

But still, Aria had to get rid of her ugly, obnoxious fur-bro. So, because love apparently makes you stupid, I asked. But not my father, because he would've said no. Just a flat-out no. And I didn't ask my mother either, because she would've told me to ask my father. So I went to the only other person who both my mother and father listened to. Gammy.

And Gammy said yes. Then told me not to tell my folks. Made me promise. So imagine their surprise when Aria showed up at my door, dog in arms. Maestro rubbing her back. Her little sister mumbling the most beautiful *I'm sorry* I ever heard.

'Gammy,' I called over my shoulder. 'Aria's here.' I welcomed her into the house.

'Aria, wait,' Maestro said, setting the dog's crate down on the porch so he could pull a disposable camera from his back pocket.

'Dad, I'm not in the mood for pictures. Seriously.'

'Then just let me get one of Jeremy,' he said, turning the exposure wheel. Once loaded, he held the camera up to his face and snapped a photo. 'Let me get one more.'

'Dad.' The look on Aria's face was enough for Maestro to return his camera to his pocket.

'Okay, okay. Well . . . we'll be back in an hour to get you,' Maestro said, gripping Aria's shoulders. Turtle gave Aria the biggest hug her little arms could manage, then she and Maestro turned back toward the car.

My mother had just gotten home from the shop, and my father was getting ready to leave for the bingo hall. Gammy was coming from the living room. They all, by chance, met in the foyer where me and Aria and Jeremy were.

'Oh, hey, Aria,' my mother said.

'Aria the *star*-ia,' my dad said, because he's a dad.

'Is this *him*?' Gammy said. That's it. Gammy came sliding forward with her arms outstretched like a zombie, reaching for the dog, who contorted himself in Aria's arms.

'Is who, who?' my father said, reaching for his jacket, which hung on the coatrack in the corner to the left of the front door. The coatrack only he used.

'Oh, this is Jeremy.' Aria stroked the pup's head, trying to calm him down.

'And Jeremy is coming to live with us for a while,' Gammy concluded. My father immediately put his jacket back on the hook as Ma squawked, *'What?'*

'Yep!' Gammy took Jeremy into her arms as if she'd been handed a newborn from a nurse. And . . . Jeremy didn't bark. Jeremy stopped squirming and just nestled into the crook of Gammy's arms.

And ten minutes later my grandmother was laughing. And ten minutes after that my parents took a meeting in their bedroom. Ten minutes after that they returned to find me and Aria sitting on the couch on the other side of the room, holding hands, watching as Gammy and Jeremy slow-danced to nothing. And ten minutes after that my father huffed and puffed, a slow-spinning tornado, returned to the coatrack for his jacket but didn't bother taking it. His temperature was already too high for an extra layer. But apparently not too high to notice me and Aria's hands.

'The way I held her hand?' I asked, now even more perplexed. First of all, I ain't know Dad had even seen that because he was so mad. But also, I wasn't sure what holding my girlfriend's hand had to do with . . . anything.

'Yeah. Because it was less of a grip. More of a . . . touch,' my dad explained, paper-towelling oil residue from his fingers. 'Like, to hold a hand the way we held yours as a child, with a full grip, that feels like a gesture of safety. To hold hands with each other's fingers woven together can sometimes seem like a gesture of desperation. But the way y'all were yesterday – your pinky just barely curled around hers – well, to me, that feels . . . intimate.'

'And what, exactly, does that mean?' I asked.

'I mean . . . it's hard to explain.'

'Intimate?' I knew the word, but didn't know what it had to do with this conversation.

'No. It's hard to explain what you're feeling,' he said. 'And I know that because I've felt it with your mother. There's a tenderness you're offering her. A tenderness she offers you. And, from what I know now, there ain't much in this world sexier than that.'

I hadn't thought about it that way, but I nodded anyway. Nodded at the fact that I *did* feel like this about Aria. And that I knew she felt this way about me. And that I didn't even really remember trying to hold her finger like that. It was just a thing that happened. Maybe by happenstance. Maybe by habit. Maybe by some kind of helpless magnetism. Either way, my dad had noticed it. And now, I noticed it too.

'I say all that to say, being a virgin is a beautiful thing. And so is sex, as long as you remember what it feels like to have your finger hooked with hers,' he said, tossing the jug of oil into the recycling. 'Connection. Got me?'

'I think so.'

'Good.'

'That's it?' I asked. Was this all he was going to say?

'Yeah, that's all,' he said, squinting at me. 'What you expect me to say?'

'I don't know. Something about me . . . growing my oats. Or whatever y'all old men be talking about.'

'First of all, ain't nobody old. And second of all, it's *sowing* your oats,' he said, shaking his head.

'Yeah, that's what Grandy said.' I eyed him. 'You not gon' tell me to sleep with as many girls as possible?'

'Ha!' Dad hollered. Then he laughed naturally, and when it tapered off, he shouted again. 'Ha! Oh, Grandy.' He looked up at the ceiling, up to heaven. Then refocused on me. 'Son, you really think that's what I *want* for you?'

'Ain't that what *you* did?'

What was left of the laughter stopped. Immediately.

'Listen, my first time was with your mom. And it wasn't long after that she was pregnant, because no one was there to tell me much of nothing. Me and her broke up right after Nat's first birthday because I was busy trying to *sow my oats.* Like a dumbass. I lied about it. And it's been eighteen years since we've been back together, and I'm still apologising for it.'

This wasn't new news. I'd heard the story before, from Ma, how I was their reunion baby. But for a moment there was remorse on Dad's face. Just a flash of it dredged up from some corner of his memory. Still.

'I mean, that was a long time ago, though. Y'all were kids.' I tried to console him.

'Yeah, but what happened between us wasn't a matter of youth; it was a matter of truth. I shouldn't have lied. So no, I'm not gonna encourage you to sow oats, and I'm also not gonna tell you not to take life as it comes. I'm just gonna tell you to be honest. Through the tender moments and the tense ones.'

Dad hooked my neck, kissed my forehead.

'Hey, so, can this stay between us, please?' I asked as he pulled his face away from mine.

'Of course.' He nodded like he already knew to do so.

And as I washed and dried the cardboard dust from my hands, only to dirty them again by grabbing two of the broken-down boxes and heading for the door, Dad called out to me, his voice like a pat on the back.

'Oh, and one more thing,' he said. 'Don't bring no babies home unless they can count money.'

A hard pat, but a pat nonetheless.

• • • •

It amazes me that whenever we open, there are always so many people already lined up outside. And on Halloween, it's always wild to see so many of our regulars, waiting as usual, but dressed in the silliest costumes.

Mr Robbins was dressed as . . . Robin. Not the bird. The sidekick, which wouldn't have been a strange costume if he wasn't, like, ninety years old. Also, who dresses up as the *sidekick*? A man whose last name is . . . Robbins, that's who. By the way, last year he came as a robber. And of course, the year before that he came as . . . a robin.

Or Mr Spuddy, who was not dressed up at all, and the thing about him not being dressed up was that I wasn't going to say a word to him about it. No one was. He's one of those guys you don't play with, because if you do, things can get scary in real life. And Halloween won't be happy. The rumour about Mr Spuddy – or, as he's known in Paradise Hill, Special Force Spuddy – is that he killed a man by pressing his finger too hard against the man's forehead. They say he calls the move *the power button*, and that he can turn anyone's life off whenever he feels like it. And he looks like the kind of guy who could do that kind of thing. Wide shoulders, square jaw, bald head with a big dent on the side of it.

Mr Spuddy only comes to the bingo hall on Halloween, just so that the neighbourhood kids ain't afraid to go to his door and ask for candy from his wife. If people think he's home, nobody's knocking, too scared he'll knock someone out. Matter fact, on Halloween a few years ago, Mrs Spuddy actually had to stand outside on the curb all night long just to make sure everybody knew her husband wasn't home and wouldn't be home on Halloween going forward. Instead, he came down – was sent down – to the bingo hall, to scare the hell out of *me*.

Standing next to him was his daughter and antonym, Lana.

'Lana, what you doing here?' I asked. Lana never came. But she was with her father this time and dressed as a butterfly.

'I grew up playing bingo with him in the house and, now that I'm eighteen, wanted to see what it would be like to play in here with the real bingo bosses.'

'Wait. You played bingo in the house with . . . *him*?' I nodded at Mr Spuddy, but not before taking a step back.

She laughed. He didn't. I waved them through.

Or Mr and Mrs Harding, who came strutting through the door wearing one outfit. As in, they'd squeezed into a single shirt. They'd squeezed into a big pair of trousers. Thankfully, they had on separate pairs of shoes.

'Who y'all supposed to be?' I asked. 'Conjoined twins?'

'No,' Mrs Harding replied. And then the three of us just stood there – me, waiting for them to tell me who or what they were dressed as, and them, not telling me. Finally, I just said all awkward, 'Well, Happy Halloween!' And waved them through.

And the costumes kept coming. Mr Stallworth, fresh from praying in his car, came strutting in as a firefighter, and Mr Stanfield came hobbling in on his cane as Chewbacca. And the goblins and the gangsters and everything in between. Until a cat, a dog, a panda, and a vampire came to the door. The animal costumes were just furry pajamas, headband ears, and plastic noses strapped on by rubber bands. The cat was Savion, the dog Tuna, and the panda Fred.

Now, the vampire was decked all the way out. Wig, fangs. Suit. Cape.

'Good *eve*ning, *Ne*on.' Even had the vampire voice.

'Aria . . . where you even find this cape?' I asked, lifting my mask and throwing my arm around her.

'I made it. But this is nothing. Look at what I did for *Turtle*.' Aria opened the photos on her phone, showed me a picture of Turtle dressed in a fur coat with a matching hat, pearls around her neck, her hair curled like an old lady's. 'Took me forever, but I made all this from a fuzzy blanket my dad got from the thrift store. Made the pearls with thread and white corn kernels. She's perfect.'

'She is. But . . . who is she?'

Aria looked at me like I'd lost my mind.

'What? She's Marian Anderson. The first Black person to sing at the Metropolitan Opera.'

'How could you not see that?' Tuna teased.

'Of course.' I checked the picture again. Turned it sideways. 'I . . . I *do* see it.' I kissed Aria's hand. 'Listen, what y'all doing here?'

'What you mean?' Fred asked, his mathematical moles lifting on his forehead. 'Is it not Halloween?'

'It's obviously Halloween.'

'Is this not Neon Bingo?' Tuna asked.

'This is Neon Bingo.'

'Is your name not Neon?' Savion asked.

'You know it is.'

'Well, then, this is where we're supposed to be,' Aria said, leaning in for a peck. They'd come to surprise me. Plus, they'd always wanted to play bingo, and figured if there was ever a night they could get in and play without anyone questioning whether or not they were too young to be there, it would be the night they could be camouflaged.

'But I thought we were gonna meet about the yearbook stuff,' I said, waving them in.

'We are, we are,' Fred said. 'But what time is this over? Because I gotta pick Saskia up from church.'

'Midnight,' I said. 'But . . . tell her to save you a seat, because y'all not staying.'

'We're definitely staying,' Savion insisted, looking around. 'As a matter fact, I was thinking maybe we could take a couple pictures of you in here. That way we could highlight our lives outside of high school. "Then a ploughman said, Speak to us of Work."' Savion eased his phone from his onesie pocket.

'Is that poetry?' I asked.

'Yep.'

'Nope.' I shut it down.

'Oh, come on, it might be cool,' Aria said.

'Yeah, like a statement saying we're actually more than school,' Fred said.

'True, but it's a *school* yearbook. A documentation of *school*,' I argued.

'No, it's really a documentation of our senior year,' Savion rebutted.

'Right. Of *school*.' I put a period on it.

'But—' Savion had more to say, but I paused him.

'Y'all, y'all—' I waved other people through. Ms Whitestone, dressed as a flamingo. I thought. I turned back to my friends. 'Ain't this what the meeting was supposed to be about?'

'Well, we having it now,' said Fred.

'No, we're not, because I gotta work.' Then realising someone was missing, I added, 'Also, where's Dodie?'

'Told us he'd meet us here,' said Aria. They all shrugged.

And Dodie would meet them, meet us, there. But not until later. Not until after Aria, Fred, Savion, and Tuna had already found a table to sit at, settled in, bought their bingo cards and a few daubers, which are what the fancy stamp-markers are called.

Not until after I brought Mrs Monihan over to where they were sitting to introduce her.

'Hey, y'all, guess who this is?' I buzzed, way too excited. And before they could answer, I jumped back in with 'Dodie's grandmother!'

Not until after Mrs Monihan gave everyone a hug and rubbed everyone's hands for good luck.

Not until after the first game started. Five squares, horizontal. Simple and plain, and I was able to see everyone's daubing style. Savion was a long dauber. He'd press the tip of the dauber to the card and push until the ink completely saturated it. Fred was a drauber, meaning instead of stamping the square like everyone else, he used the dauber like a marker, and drew *X*s over each number. Tuna was as cool as Tuna always is. Dabbed like a pro. Like she had bingo in her blood. And Aria was what we call a destroyer, which just means she pounded the dauber on each square as if she were trying to kill the number printed on it.

None of them won. Priscilla Wall, dressed as Tina Turner, did. Screamed *Bingo* as if she were screaming *Fire!* Or *Help!* Or *Amen!* Or *Big wheels keep on turnin'!* And Aria, Fred, Tuna, and Savion all clapped. Which is not a thing. Ain't nobody ever happy another person wins. Not at bingo. The correct responses to a losing bingo round are silence or a low moan lasting no longer than three seconds. Just long enough for my father to announce the next game.

'Next up we're playing five squares, vertical,' my father called out from the bingo pulpit. 'Three minutes before first ball. Three minutes before first ball.'

During that three-minute hiatus, I was on. My time to get over to Priscilla and pay her winnings. The early games are low bucks. Fifty. Easy to count out. Ten five-dollar bills.

'Here's five for you,' she said, handing a bill back.

'Just under two minutes,' my father warned. 'Just under two minutes.'

And then: enter Dodie.

He burst into the room holding a bag and was dressed in what looked like a human-sized toilet-paper roll after the paper is all gone. The cardboard tube I used to pretend was a telescope. And he had a fuzzy orange hat on his head. And, of course, sunglasses. He looked around the room frantically before spotting the team, and waddled as fast as he could to the table to sit with them. Well, he couldn't really sit. So he just stood there, laid his bingo cards out, and after they were lined up, out came the action figures. Toys I'd never seen. Ever. In life. Like, I didn't recognise the heroes.

'I have questions,' Aria said, before I could say anything.

'Me too,' I said.

'All of us do.' Tuna stared at Dodie, her face evenly split between amazement and disgust. 'But I'll start. What you supposed to be?'

Dodie continued organising the table space in front of him.

'A bingo dauber,' he said, without looking up. 'Obviously.'

'How you know what a bingo' – Fred looked at the marker in front of him to make sure he got the name right – '*dauber* is?'

'A better question is, where you coming from?' Savion asked.

'My mother made me look at college applications,' Dodie said, all blasé, like college was just another thing meant to take up his precious time.

'*You* going to college?' Tuna jumped at the chance to snap on him.

'I don't know. I think my mother just wants me out the house,' Dodie said. 'Y'all know how it is.'

'I sure do,' Aria chimed in. 'And I can't wait to be out. I'm only applying to places far, far away from here.'

'Ouch.' I didn't mean to say it. It was like my mouth spoke what my body felt. A sucker punch.

'From her, babe. I meant to say, away from *her*.' Aria grabbed my hand.

'I know, and it's cool,' I assured her.

'You thinking about going with her, Nee?' This from Savion, who I knew without asking would be going to school on a wrestling scholarship. We all knew that.

'Nah, I don't think college, at least regular college, is my thing.' I shrugged.

'And it don't have to be,' Aria said, now squeezing my hand.

'Thirty seconds!' Dad called out.

'Yeah, I'm just gonna hold down the fort here. Answer any questions people might have about how my genius girlfriend is doing.' I smiled. It was halfway forced. But I meant it, and I hoped – and still hope – it comes true.

'Aww.' Aria's love-whimper eased some of my anxiety around it all. 'Well, I'll tell you what I wish. I wish . . . someone would answer a question for me right now about our, uh, *genius* friend, Dodie,' she tacked on, watching as Dodie continued to set the toys up.

'*Genius* must have a new definition, and I just ain't smart enough to know it,' Tuna jabbed. 'Seriously, Dodo, what *is* all this?'

Dodie didn't pay us no attention. Too busy concentrating

on getting himself prepped as quickly as possible. The rest of the room had settled and was waiting on my father, who'd begun to spin the cage.

'Game two. Game number two. Here comes the first ball,' Dad said through the speakers. 'O41. The first ball is O41.'

Everyone started daubing in their own way. Except Dodie, who pulled out an ink pen and drew zigzags through his O41 box.

'Where's your . . . thing?' Savion asked.

'Don't got one,' Dodie said. 'Keeping it punk.'

'But you dressed like—'

'Shh!' Dodie said as my father called out the next number.

In between each game, I'd run to do the payments and run back to try to meet about yearbook stuff the best we could.

'What number he just said?' Savion asked.

'N7, I think,' Aria said, before getting back to business. 'All we need to decide tonight is how to divvy up responsibilities. Who gon' do what?'

'None of y'all that smart—' Fred declared, or at least tried to.

'*Who* ain't that smart?' Aria warned.

'I didn't mean it like that,' Fred clarified. 'I'm talking about when it comes to coding. So I'll do all that stuff.'

'And I'll write all the captions,' Savion said.

'I'll do the music,' Dodie said.

'What number was that?' From Savion again.

'I38,' Tuna confirmed, searching her card. 'And this a yearbook, not a song, Dodo.'

'Everything's a song, Tuna,' Dodie shot back. 'Plus, this ain't no regular yearbook. It's a year . . . site.'

'Still not a song, but whatever,' she rumbled, realising she didn't have I38.

'No, he's right. A soundtrack might be cool. Because this is different. So we can be creative,' I said.

'But the same,' Aria chimed in. 'Like, I think I want to come up with some superlatives. But better ones than just *Best Dressed* or *Class Clown*.' Aria turned to me. 'What you gon' do, babe?'

I wasn't sure. And this wasn't really the best place to

brainstorm because I was trying to pay attention to all them while also listening for bingo.

'B11,' Dad called. Then repeated, 'B11.'

I shrugged. I honestly didn't know what I could do, and . . . my father was right. I'd joined just because Aria said it was a good idea.

'I mean, you know how to do a lot of good stuff.' Aria, full of encouragement.

'Being a boyfriend ain't a yearbook role,' Fred joked.

'Whatever. I can take pictures,' I said. 'Oh, you know what would be even better? Videos. Like, little movies or something.'

'G18,' my father said.

'Videos?' Savion said.

'Bingo!' Dodie screamed.

'Bingo!' Another voice came from the other side of the room. A hand went up.

'We have two winners!' my father howled. 'Bingo, bingo!'

Dodie waddled a few steps from the table to see who the other winner was. Who he'd be splitting the pot with.

'Who's that?' he asked as I counted out his money. Two

forty in twenties. He put the whole thing in his bag. No tip. I turned to see who he was asking about.

'Oh, that's Lana. You know Mr Spuddy, who lives up the block from me? That's his daughter.' Dodie pulled one of the twenties out from the fold in his bag, scribbled his name, number, and a note on it.

'Swap me out,' he said, slick. I gave him a clean twenty from the payout stash for his scribbled one. 'Now she's really a winner.' A collective groan from the table.

'Dodie!' Another voice. A familiar one. An older one. One that almost caused him to jump out his . . . tube. His grandmother Mrs Monihan, her hand in the air, beckoning him over. He sulked, went, and a few minutes later returned with his granny beside him.

'She wants to sit with us,' he growled.

For the rest of the night we all laughed and played and watched Dodie squirm as we talked with his grandmother.

'Y'all so fun!' she said, slapping the table. 'I can't believe y'all spending your Halloween in here with us. Y'all young. Supposed to be out there acting up.'

'Not us, Grandma,' Dodie said like a little boy, and

everyone at the table smiled like angels. Even though it was a lie. I mean, last Halloween we were all partying at Dorian Blankenship's house, which, if Aria's house is in a graham-cracker neighbourhood, Dorian's looks like it's made of those wafer-sandwich-cookie things that taste just sweet enough to not be paper. Gammy loves those because they're easy on her teeth. They disintegrate in her mouth. The point is, Dorian's neighbourhood looks like a neighbourhood of delicate castles.

I'd had to work, as usual. Was fully dressed as Wolverine, which was a bad idea because it was impossible to count out the money with the claws. But what made up for that was that Nat and Spank spent Halloween at the hall too. Nat knew I wanted to go see Aria, so she let me drop them off at Spank's house so I could take the car to Dorian's. I swear, I barely saw a little bit of Dorian's house – area rugs everywhere – before me and Aria saw a lot of the inside of Nat's car. But we just fooled around, kissed and touched and wished we could do more than kiss and touch but knew we weren't ready to do more than kiss and touch. And the next morning Nat swore her car smelled like breath. Like deep breath. Breath so deep, the vanilla tree couldn't even mask it. I still haven't lived that down.

'Not y'all, huh?' Mrs Monihan replied, now looking at us like she knew that wasn't true. Because she knew that wasn't true. Because she knew her grandson was a liar, which led her into telling stories about who Dodie was as a kid. Even told the one about the sunglasses.

Mrs Monihan didn't win no games, and none of us besides Dodie did either. But that was okay, because even though teasing Dodie was a blast, the best thing about her sitting with us, for me, was when she started talking about her husband, Ronald, and their way of loving each other.

'He never said too much, even when our love was new and sweet, when it was still puppy love,' she explained. 'Not like my grandson here.'

'But everybody always says communication is the key to . . . everything,' Aria said, her hand resting on mine.

'Oh, it is. It is. But Ronald always felt like everything that needed to be said could be said in three words. "I am mad. I want more. I'm so sorry. You hurt me. You look great. I need help."'

Three words. That's it. And that was it. That conversation was what sparked me. Helped me figure out the prompt for the yearbook recordings. And after the final game and everyone had filed out of the bingo hall, I began, first recording the people right in front of me.

State your name.

Fred Creeks.

How would you describe high school in three words?

A good time.

A good time? That's it?

A blessed *time.*

State your name.

Savion Gunther.

How would you describe high school in three words?

Hmmm. I think for me it would be something like . . .

Mind your business.

Word.

Why you looking at me like that?

I just wasn't expecting that. Thought you'd say something

about wrestling. Like, No holds barred or something like that.

That's a good one, but nah. It's definitely Mind your business.

State your name.

Petunia Randolph. Tuna.

How would you describe high school in three words?

I guess it would have to be Everything works out.

Everything works out?

I hope so.

Where Dodie at?

Who cares?

State your name.

Aria Wright, aka Aria the star-ia, coming to you live from the parking lot of Neon Bingo.

Okay, okay. How would you describe high school in three words?

Should've been first.

I know, but you were in there talking to my dad.

He loves me.

Are those your three words?

Nope. My three words are Should've been first.

She gazed into the camera. That look. And I suddenly wondered what we were talking about.

Should be first, she repeated, this time with a slight edit. And suddenly, I knew what we were talking about. At least, I thought I did.

Can be first, I replied, then stopping the recording, realising our interview was becoming a conversation. A special conversation.

'Will be first.' Aria smiled, pinky up.

And twenty-four months before that . . .

I was at my grandfather's funeral. Crying. His wallet had been given to me by my grandmother just before the ceremony started. She said he wanted me to have it. Cards, photos, receipts, a few bucks, and whatever else was in it. It felt heavy in my back pocket, too full for a kid my age.

> *Earl Wednesday died on October 23 after suffering a heart attack in the shop that he owned and worked at for over fifty years, where he provided upwards of ten thousand homes with door knockers. He was a loving husband to Sharletta Wednesday, a committed father to Brina Benton, and the grandfather of Natalie and Neon Benton, whom he spoiled. His hobbies were sleeping; enjoying*

terrible-smelling, slow-burning cigars; purposely wrinkling his clothes; talking trash; and watching movies with his grandson. His favourite actor was Denzel Washington. His favourite movie snack . . . French fries.

The obituary said more, but that was my favourite part. After reading it, Reverend Creeks gave a sermon about love and respect, which my grandfather stood for, but also how his work as a beloved and disciplined door-knocker maker was finally over.

'Yes, what a noble job to be a maker of door knockers on this earth,' the reverend said, dabbing sweat from his forehead. 'To encourage people to knock and wait before entering the dwelling places of friends, family, and strangers is nothing short of the Lord's work. But in heaven . . .'

The organ player began to play.

'*Oh*, in heaven . . .' Reverend Creeks tightened his own spring. He clapped his hands together. 'I said, in *heaven* . . .' More organ, and more moaning from the congregation. My grandmother stood up, put her hand in the air as if trying to high-five the reverend. Or Jesus. Or Grandy. 'In heaven, those big, pearly gates don't need no knocker! That doorway to forever don't need nothing built from a brass mould! You know why?'

'Why?' We all threw it back at him.

'I said, you know why?'

'Why?!' we said louder.

'Because God broke the mould!' Lightning on the organ. Thunder in the pews. My grandmother looked like she was going to start jumping up and down, which I was scared about because her knees and hips, though good for walking, might not have been so good for jumping. The preacher preached on. 'No, I'm happy to say brother Earl's job is all done, because there's no need to knock when God's door is always wide open. God was just waiting on Earl *Wednesday* to get on over that *hump*, to arrive!'

More everything. Organ. Handclaps. Stomps. Tambourine. Amen, amen, amen. Nat put her arm around me and squeezed tight.

After the funeral, Nat would continue to hold me as we all piled into cars and paraded through town, down to the cemetery so that we could say our final goodbyes before they lowered Grandy's casket into the ground. For me, there was a strangeness to the permanence of it all. That my grandfather's body would go into the dirt and there was no digging it back up. And even if I tried, which I, of course, wouldn't, but even if I did, he wouldn't be in there. Not as I knew him. Nature would've already changed him.

I didn't want to see the lowering or even be that close to the casket. So Nat stood off to the side with me, her arm still draped over my shoulder. Though we couldn't see Gammy's and our parents' faces from where we were standing, we could still tell Gammy was struggling. Broken. She rested her head on my mother's shoulder, and my father had his log of an arm stretched across the backs of them both.

If this were a movie, then this would be when it would begin to rain. The black umbrellas would appear, blooming like flowers of gloom. And the black sheep of the family would be standing far away from everyone else, looking on, taking swigs from a pint bottle. But I wasn't no black sheep. I was just a fifteen-year-old boy, standing back, wondering who I'd argue with about whether or not Denzel should do more romances.

My grandfather thought so. He believed this with every fibre of his being, which seems like such a silly argument to have to that extent. But he did. All the time. With me.

'Listen, I know he's good at action films,' Grandy would say. 'I mean, the man done played every military officer there is to play. And I know he's good at drama. You name it, a jazz musician, an attorney, a basketball player, and even a detective, he's good. But I don't know if you can really be *great* if you can't . . . do . . . romance.'

Grandy had this way of saying a thing as if it were true because he'd said it. And he'd keep a cigar tucked in the corner of his mouth, which, for some reason, always added to the image of him being an expert.

'I disagree,' I'd say, straight up and down.

'That's because you ain't lived long enough!' Grandy would bark. And then he'd tell me his own story. A story I'd heard enough times to recite. 'You know what I was doing before I took over my daddy's business with all this door-knocker mess? I was in the army. Got in at eighteen and got shipped straight off to war. And when people would shoot in my direction, I had brothers with me, my comrades, who would cover my back and handle what I didn't see coming. Now, you could argue that they saved my life. Maybe. But they *definitely* saved my body.' He'd take a pull on his cigar, let the smoke ghost from his mouth before continuing. 'And when I got back all traumatised and triggered, my daddy gave me an opportunity to train to be a door-knocker maker. It was hard work. Long days. And was never nothing I saw myself doing despite my father owning the business. On top of that, it seemed to take me forever to get the hang of it. But when I did, it provided me an opportunity to make money and support myself. Some might argue that door knockers saved my life. Maybe. But it *certainly* saved my mind.' He'd take another puff. A shorter one. Like a kiss. 'But when I met your grandmother in that laundromat all them years ago, and we started dating, oh, Nee . . . I ain't never been more sure that her love saved my *life*.'

'But how?' I always asked. 'What makes you think that?'

'Because it was the only time I ain't have to act like anyone other than myself,' he said, pinching a stray bit of tobacco off his tongue. 'And that's why I want to see Denzel do more romance. See if he could bring that to the people. I know he knows it. Been in love for decades. Matter fact . . . I got just the role for him. He could play me!'

Was what I was thinking about, trying not to watch what everyone else was watching.

Or when we'd go to the gas station to get five dollars' worth of gas, five dollars he'd pull from that old sweat-worn wallet bursting at the seams. And another buck or two to buy a few boxes of matches for his cigars. This was always when I'd catch him looking at some woman, admiring her beauty. I remember once he watched a woman walk halfway down the block and wouldn't even close his wallet until he couldn't see her anymore, as if he were waiting for her to double back and ask him for money. And when she was far enough, he closed it and returned the leather hunk to his back pocket and put his eyes on me.

'Pretty, right?' he asked, patting my shoulder.

'Yeah.'

'Yeah, well, one of these days your daddy's probably gon' tell you some stupid shit about sowing your oats. His daddy taught him that, and his daddy before that. Shit, my daddy definitely said it a time or two to me when I was your age.'

'And what does that mean?' I asked, refraining from asking if it had anything to do with oatmeal or farming, both of which I ain't care nothing about.

'Getting all you can, and canning all you get,' Grandy said, gruff.

'O . . . kay, and what does *that* mean?' Seriously, why do grandfathers speak in riddles?

'It means when you finally get you some, go get you some more. And some more. And some more. Until you've had enough running around, and you're ready to settle down,' Grandy explained, shaking the matchbox like palm peanuts. We were standing outside the truck, waiting for the gas pump to click. 'But . . . that's bullshit.'

'So, I *shouldn't* do that?' *Click.*

'I'm not saying what you should or shouldn't do, grandson. It's your life. I'm just telling you, the desire for more don't die.' Grandy pointed to the pump with his chin. I pulled it from the tank, set it in its holster. We both got back in the truck. 'You know, I've been eating birthday cake my whole damn life, and every single birthday party, I want another piece. Whether it's my birthday or yours.' He laughed, pulling out of the station. 'So I'd be a fool to wait for the urge to go away before I start monitoring my sugar. Gotta exercise some self-control. Understand?'

Was what I was also thinking about.

Or when he'd pick me up from school in the eighth grade, and I'd go into his glove compartment and pull out his cologne and spritz myself because I wanted to smell like him. A combination of spice and something else. Maybe wood. Maybe smoke, but not the cigar smoke. Some other kind of better-smelling smoke. And one day I went looking for it and the bottle was gone, replaced by a washcloth and a bar of soap.

'Soap and water is undefeated,' he said. 'But like everything in life, you gotta know how to use 'em.'

'I know how to wash, Grandy. I just like to—'

'Your mother told me you ain't getting to it.' He coughed the words at me.

I sucked my teeth, annoyed, thinking Ma told him about how a few nights before, she'd scrubbed my neck with cotton balls to show me my own dirt.

'Me and her already did this, though. I'm good now.'

'I hear you,' Grandy said, which meant he either hadn't heard, or had and didn't care. 'But do you know how to wash your ass?'

'Come on, Grandy. I just said I know how to wash.'

'Okay, okay. I'm just saying, not only is cleanliness next to godliness, uncleanliness is next to no one.'

Was what I was thinking about. At the grave site. While my feet crunched under the fallen leaves, the sound of cracking seemed like an appropriate soundtrack. While my grandmother and mother wept. While Reverend Creeks read Scripture and said the Lord's Prayer. While a few soldiers presented Gammy with a folded American flag.

Until the sound of a barking dog unfolded the moment.

I turned to my right – no dog there. Then to my left, trying to figure out which direction the bark was coming from, and why it seemed to be getting closer, and why there was a voice following the bark, someone calling after the dog.

'Jeremy! Jeremy, stop! Stop, Jeremy!' And before I knew it, he was right on me. A little thing, no bigger than a shoe, darting through the cemetery, over the hills of tombstones, straight toward me.

And I did what I'd always done when it came to dogs. Ran.

First around the canopy where my grandfather and family were. But the dog followed, woofing like a coughing old man, my family jolted out of their mourning, disrupted by the mayhem. Then I jetted across the field, trying not to step on any fresh plots or flowers as the dog continued to chase me. The girl running behind us, calling for it but also screaming for me to stop running. But I couldn't. I just couldn't. But what I did do was circle back and lead the dog right toward her.

'Get him! Get him! Get him!' I cried, dashing past her in a blur. And she did. Scooped the dog into her arms as I ran a few more paces before realising I was safe.

I folded over, my body doing its best to snatch air.

'I'm so sorry,' the girl cried out, her feet coming into my sight line. Because I was still hunched over, staring at the ground, the grass void of blades, everything green waterco-lour. 'I'm so, so sorry,' she repeated.

I nodded. Straightened up. Rested my arms on top of my head. My dress shirt had come loose from my trousers. The waxy laces of my church shoes untied.

'I was trying to put the leash on him, but he broke away. Jumped right out the car,' she explained. And then I looked at her. And could finally see her. Sweatpants. T-shirt. Ponytail. Perfect.

'It's okay,' I managed to get out. 'Forreal, it's fine.'

'I'm . . . um . . . gonna go apologise to your family,' she said, looking embarrassed. At first I wasn't sure that was a good idea, but when we got a little closer to the casket and canopy, Gammy and Ma and Nat and everyone else were all laughing.

'Boy, if that ain't a sign from your granddaddy, I don't know what is.' Gammy cackled.

'A sign of . . . what?' I asked, my body still levelling out.

'A sign to tell us to get going. And keep going. You know he never liked no whole bunch of sadness,' she said. 'So, young lady and Mr Pup, thank you.'

'What's your name, sweetheart?' Ma asked, one arm rubbing Gammy's back.

'Aria. And this troublemaker is Jeremy.'

'Well, Aria, I'm Mrs Benton, and this near victim is my son, Neon.'

'Hi,' I said, suddenly wishing this were *my* funeral.

'Hey.' Aria extended her hand, but the moment I went to shake it, Jeremy barked.

'Oh, shush,' Aria said, bouncing the dog like a baby. 'He's okay. He's okay.' I took my hand back. Put it in my pocket.

'You live over here, Aria?' Gammy chimed in.

'No, I live in Kingman Park. But my dad had to come over this way to pick up a . . . a door knocker or something. Some kind of thing for the door. But the place was closed.'

My grandmother's eyes wet up. So did my mother's. Then Ma scratched her head.

'A door knocker?' my mother asked. 'What kinda door knocker, sweetie?'

'It's a . . . whole note.'

• • • •

Because my grandfather prided himself on good customer service and my mother prides herself on it even more, once the funeral was over and everything was wrapped up, Ma went into the shop, pulled Mr Wright's name from her records, called him and apologised for not being open when he came by for his door knocker – *Mr Wednesday passed away* – and told him that to make up for the inconvenience, she would have it delivered. She offered *me* up as messenger. He agreed. And the following Saturday I found myself on the bus with a brass whole note, which I had no idea about, wrapped in tissue paper and boxed up beautifully.

When I finally made it to Kingman Park, I took my time admiring the houses, all of which were very different than the ones in Paradise Hill. If Paradise Hill was a little bit of everything, Kingman Park was a lot of bit of the same thing. And that thing, was perfection. Grass two inches high. Clean, fancy cars in the driveway. Welcome mats that said WELCOME. Hedges. Not bushes, hedges.

I'd check the address occasionally. Then check the house

numbers, each house looking like the last house, which looked like the last house, which looked like the last.

Until.

873 Kingman Park Drive. I double-checked. Triple-checked. This was the house. It was green. Well, half-green. A man stood on a ladder, painting over the green with yellow.

'Excuse me,' I called out. But the man didn't hear me over the sounds coming from inside the house. A duet of trumpet and *arf*. So I came closer to the ladder. 'Excuse me!'

'Oh!' he said, startled. 'You scared me. How you doing, young man?'

'I'm fine. Um . . . I'm looking for Mr . . .' I checked the paper. 'Mr Wright.'

'Maestro,' he said, pointing to himself. 'And you found him.'

Maestro eased down the ladder.

'I came to deliver your order from Wednesday's Door Knockers,' I explained.

'Ah, I've been waiting for this,' he said, his feet now on the ground. 'By the way, my condolences. Your grandfather was a good man.' He set the paintbrush on the ground across the top of the paint can and took the box. He threw the lid on the grass, then began peeling back the tissue paper, and the music (and the barking) got louder. Because the front door had been opened.

Aria came from the house dressed in overalls. In her hand, a paintbrush.

'Hey,' she said, making her way over to where me and her father stood.

'Aria, you know . . .'

'Neon.'

'Neon,' Maestro said, holding up the untissued door knocker. Then he thought about it. *'Neon?'*

'Yes sir. Neon,' I confirmed.

'I met him the other day when Jeremy got loose,' Aria said. 'Again, I'm so, so sorry. That was . . . wild.'

'Yeah,' I said. 'It's cool. I wasn't scared or nothing like that. Just caught off guard, y'know?'

Aria looked at me. Looked. Looked. Looked. Then made a sound like she was holding in a sneeze. But it wasn't a sneeze. It was a laugh.

'I'm serious,' I said. And I was. Maybe not honest, but definitely serious. Aria just nodded, clearly afraid that if she opened her mouth, a howl would come out.

'Okay, okay,' Aria finally said, still holding back. I waited for her to say something else, but she didn't. At least not immediately. Instead, she just tucked her brush in her pocket, picked up her father's, and started dabbing the lower parts of the house. Maestro had taken the door knocker inside. Hadn't returned just yet.

'You know this would've been much easier if y'all painted over the green with white first, right?' I learned that from my dad. He paints the inside walls of the bingo hall once a year. Doing it this way was going to take forever. They would need a bunch of coats for the green to not bleed through.

She looked at me like I'd said something wrong. And for a moment, I thought maybe I had.

'Here,' she said, handing me the second paintbrush. The one she had tucked down in the pocket of her overalls.

'What you want me to do with this?' I asked.

'Come on, you gotta paint better than you fib.'

'Paint?' I thought she was joking. I mean, my father painted, but *I'd* never painted a day in my life.

'Or . . . leave,' Aria said, and I wasn't sure if she was joking or not. She pointed to the house. 'I'm not trying to be rude, but we're obviously in the middle of something, and there's a ton left to do.'

I nodded. And stayed. First time for everything.

In the process of making the green house yellow is when I learned that me and Aria went to the same school and that we were in the same grade, but she was in all the genius classes, which was why I never saw her. I learned that she wasn't an athlete or in any of the social clubs, or in student government, or nothing like that. Just an over-achieving academic who seemed to not give a shit about being one. School was easy for her. Almost like it was just something to do.

I also learned why they, and now *we,* were painting the house in the first place.

'My little sister likes yellow at the moment. So . . . we painting it yellow for now,' Aria said with a shrug.

'That's it? That's the only reason?'

'Yep. That's it,' she said. But that was because she hadn't known me yet. Later, as in much later, Aria told me that even though it was true that her little sister sometimes got stuck on colours and sounds – the whole hearing-colours thing – the other reason they always went along with the house painting was because her father was always trying to figure out ways to spend time outside the house to explain why things were the way they were inside. Why her mother was the way her mother was. How betrayal could make you scared, especially for your children. But, like I said, that came later. For now it was just small talk.

'Who playing that music?' I asked.

'I'm pretty sure it's my turn for a question.' Aria dipped the brush in the yellow paint, pressed it against the edge of the can to skim the excess. 'Your name really Neon?'

'Why, you don't like it?'

'Hmm, I haven't decided yet.'

'Well, I don't like it. I mean, I like it more now than I did when I was younger. But . . . I don't know. My mother says it's because she always wanted me to know I can glow in the dark,' I explained.

'Damn. I wasn't expecting that. *That*, I like.'

'But that ain't the real reason. Or the only reason. The other thing about my name is that my dad wanted to name me Neon because his name's Deon and his father's name was Leon. So . . . I got stuck with Neon, which I guess ain't as bad as it could've been.'

'Yeah, you could've been Peon.' Aria smiled.

'Exactly.'

We went on painting until my mother pulled up unexpectedly because it had gotten late and I hadn't called. Ma asked Aria about Jeremy, then spoke to Maestro for a bit, showed him where the door knocker should be positioned on their front door.

'Why y'all call this eye a whole note?' I asked, minding grown folks' business.

Aria hissed with amusement. I had no idea what I'd said, but I suddenly knew it was stupid. 'Aww. That's . . . cute.'

She didn't say it mean. There was more surprise in her *cute*, as if somehow her eyes had reset, and I was suddenly . . . cute. Like, cute in *that* way.

'Did I say something wrong?' I asked.

'I don't think so,' Aria piped up, turning toward her father, the sarcasm underneath each word aimed at him.

'Good question, young man,' Maestro said. 'A whole note is a musical note that lasts for four counts. Like this.' He hummed and tapped his foot four times to demonstrate. 'It represents the four of us in this house. A family. Whole.'

To that, Aria folded her arms. Didn't say nothing, just hugged herself.

'Oh, that's cool. Sorry.' I tried to tamp my embarrassment.

'Don't be. It was a mistake. And I think there's melody in mistakes.' Maestro turned to the door knocker, bounced his shoulder. 'I mean, it does look kinda like an eye. And I like that too.'

Maestro and my mother shook hands, and she summoned me to the car. Me and Aria said goodbye but didn't exchange numbers or nothing. And even though we went to the same school, I didn't see her again for months.

Until February.

• • • •

The only reason I joined the wrestling team was because of this kid named Curtis Whitestone. He . . . 'encouraged' me, even though it didn't feel like encouragement at the time. See, Curtis was a junior, built like a video game villain. And before he beat the brakes off me at the end of my freshman year, I thought he was cool. I thought we were cool. But Curtis ain't think it was cool that his mother gave all her money to my father every night, trying to hit bingo, which led to them being behind on rent.

But I ain't know about that until he told me. And when he told me, I felt bad. And when he told me to get his money back, I told him I couldn't. Too bad. And when he told me that since I couldn't get his money back, he'd have to beat the brakes off me, I told him nothing. And when he told me to meet him at Paradise Hill Park after school, I told him I'd be there. Like I was bad. Even though I wasn't. And I didn't want to go. But did, with Nat. And tried to look bad.

It was all bad.

So to not feel that kind of bad again, the first thing I did at the beginning of sophomore year was join the wrestling team. Not because I wanted to learn how to defend myself – though that was part of it – but because I wanted people to know I was on the wrestling team and that I was engaged in combat daily. And that I had teammates who were much better than me, one becoming one of my closest friends. Savion. And all this was enough for people like Curtis Whitestone to not try me again, no matter how much money his mother lost.

Three months into the season, which was the following February and also happened to be four months after meeting Aria and never seeing her again, I had a wrestling match. We were up against Fosterbridge High, a school known for wrestling, unlike our school, which was known mainly for basketball and Savion, who was ranked fourth in the country. My match was against a kid named . . . I don't remember his first name, but I remember his last name was Washington, because there's no way I could ever forget a Washington. I was wrestling in the 160-pound weight class (was having a growth spurt), but the Washington kid's 160 looked much different than mine. I stepped out on the mat, made sure my headgear was tight, got in my stance, shook his hand. And. *Whistle!* And. I was on my back before I could blink. He shot, took my legs out, and as I fought to keep my shoulder blades off the mat, I glanced into the crowd and saw . . . her. Aria. She'd come in with Savion's friend Brandon and was holding a greasy box of food.

She sat down on the bleachers. Looked at me, then didn't.

The whistle blew. I made it out of the first round, barely, but wouldn't make it through the second. Not uncommon for me.

After the meet I looked for her. Searched the stands and snaked through the crowd but couldn't find her until I went outside. She was hugging Brandon and congratulating Savion as they left.

'Hey.' I stopped her just before she turned to head out.

'Oh! Hey,' she said, patting me on the arm. 'Good game.'

'It was a match.'

'Right. Good match.' She gave me an ironic thumbs-up.

I smirked. 'I guess.'

'No, I'm kidding, it wasn't a good match or a good game. You got your ass beat pretty bad out there, kid,' she said, joking. 'But it should be noted, for the record, you didn't look terrible losing.' She extended what was left of the box of food. In it, a few chicken tenders, and a handful of cold fries.

'Thanks,' I said, clawing at the fries, her sense of humour making the cold and gummy consistency bearable. 'How's . . .'

'Jeremy?' She smiled.

'Yeah, Jeremy,' I replied. 'Your furry brother.'

'Oh, you know, mostly bark and very little bite.'

'A little bite is sometimes enough,' I said. Secretly, I was trying not to get too gassed off that one good line, because if I did, there wouldn't be a follow-up. I'd be one and done, thrown off my square by being surprised by my own charisma.

'That's true,' Aria said, closing the box. She looked to the left as if she were looking for someone. Waiting for someone.

'Um . . . how's the house?' I asked, trying not to lose her.

'Still yellow,' she said. 'For now.'

'For *now*?'

'Yeah. The other day, my little sister said she thinks it might sound better pink. So me and my dad are gearing up for that.'

I couldn't imagine a pink house. Especially in that neighbourhood. And I was so baffled at the thought of a pink house that I totally missed that she'd said *sound better pink*. But the thought of the pink house made me grin. Maybe because someone chose something different. Something interesting. Something bold. Something special.

And with a movie and ice cream date in mind, I asked, 'You think you might need an extra hand?'

Aria looked me in the eyes.

'Maybe.'

And she meant that *maybe*. Because even though I helped her paint the house, our first date – the movie and ice cream – didn't happen for another three months.

We saw *Purple Rain*. And ate butter pecan.

• • • •

If this were a movie, this would be the beginning of a roller-coaster relationship. There would be scenes of us at the park, laid out, reading, flowers in full bloom all around. Or walking down dampened streets at night, arm in arm, cheek to cheek. We'd cook together, which would always lead to food fights, just messy enough to be cute. I'd leave love notes for her everywhere. And she would do the same, misting them with her perfume, kissing them to leave her lip print at the bottom, where'd she'd sign her name with a heart above the *i*.

If this were a movie, all this would happen thirty minutes before I cheated on her. Maybe at a . . . Halloween party. One of the ones where the cops don't break it up. And she'd slap me. And storm out the house, and I'd run after her with a bedsheet wrapped around my waist. I'd call her phone a million times until her sister answered and told me she didn't want to talk to me. So I'd show up at her house and be threatened by her father. But when I was leaving, I'd notice her in the window.

If this were a movie, of course, we'd be an hour in by this point, and she would've moved on. There would be a new boy in her life who everyone liked but her. And I would pick a fight with him. And she would break it up, and be even more disappointed in me. She'd call me selfish and unfair. And she'd be right. And the girl at the party, the one I cheated on Aria with, would wonder why I just wouldn't get with her. Why I wouldn't commit to the fling. And so I do. Until I don't. And that's a weird conversation.

If this were a movie, this is when the subplot would take over. And I'd be consumed and distracted with something else. Maybe I move out of town. Maybe my mother falls sick. Maybe I change my mind again and decide to marry the other girl, the one from the party, and we'd start a family. And it would be beautiful. Until one day I'd bump into Aria at a coffee shop, or a yoga studio, or the gym, or the swim class our kids attend, or the grocery store, and decide that we can't blow our lives up and try again. For ten minutes. And then we'd blow our lives up and try again.

If this were a movie, Denzel Washington would not be in it.

But this ain't no movie.

This was real life. And the beginning of a special, regular story where two people meet and help each other make something beautiful, at the risk of making a mess.

No, this ain't no movie. This is a mirror. This me. This her. This us.

This is real.

Back to now . . .

Get out your head.

Count to ten. One more time.

Get out your head.

Deep breath.

Eight, nine, ten.

Deep breath.

Deep breath.

This is real.

I turn away from the mirror, from the dog, and open the bathroom door. Take the short walk across the hall to Aria's bedroom. She's sitting on the bed, but stands when she sees me. Dazzling. Still. The lamp is on, casting orange across her skin. The music is a melody I don't recognise. She's cracked a window, just barely. The spring air feels nice.

'You okay?' she asks, the faintest shiver in her voice. And all of a sudden I think of the last two years. How . . . regular it's been. Not the right word. How . . . natural. How lucky I am.

'I'm . . . a little nervous,' I say.

She nods and gives a nervous grin that softens as I grin back. She reaches her arms behind her back, undoes her bra.

Deep breath.

I follow her lead, push my underwear to the floor.

Deep breath.

She follows my follow, pushes her underwear to the floor.

Deep breath.

'Me too,' she says. And I wish I had synesthesia. Wish I could taste those five letters. I know they're sweet. Sweeter than I don't know what.

And now my breathing begins to even. Which is odd.

'Also,' Aria continues, 'while you were in there, I, um . . . I figured out my three words.'

I smile. There is a trumpet oozing low through the speakers.

'I've known mine for a long time,' I confess. I say the thing.

And in that moment, I extend my pinky, reach out for her. She meets my hand with hers, locks her little finger in mine. Tonight,

we are hooked. We pull each other. Me and Aria. Meet in the middle. Of ourselves. As ourselves. Closer than close. And softly, softly, softly, almost as if our breath has perforated, as if we are vibrating, we whisper a laugh into each other's ears.

Acknowledgements

Twenty-four seconds from now, you'll still be feeling what you're hopefully feeling at this moment. And if this book works, what you're feeling is tender and honest and like you're part of a larger community of people who desire tenderness and honesty. Hold on to that. Thank yourself for it. I've certainly thanked myself for it.

Aside from me, I'd also like to thank Alice Swan and the whole Faber family, as well as my agent, Elena Giovinazzo. Without you believing in my wild ideas, none of this would happen.

I want to thank my friends who let me ask them personal questions about their first times and all the people we experienced those first times with.

For all the people who extended me grace and patience as a teenager figuring out how to be myself with confidence and grace, thank you.

For the adults who will use this story to engage in conversation with their young people to make space for one of the most transformative times in their lives, thank you.

For the young lovers, who want to know what it is to feel safe and joyous while stumbling through maturation, thank you.

But more importantly . . . you're welcome.

Pinkies,
Jason

PS: Black boys deserve love stories too.

WHEN I WAS THE GREATEST
Indie Book Awards WINNER Children's Fiction
JASON REYNOLDS
WINNER – CILIP CARNEGIE MEDAL
Illustrated by AKHRAN GIRMAY
'Moving and thought-provoking.' Kirkus
'A rewarding read.' Publisher's Weekly, Starred Review
'Unexpectedly gorgeous.' Booklist

A lot of the stuff that gives my neighbourhood a bad name, I don't really mess with.

Ali's got enough going on, between school and boxing and helping out at home. His best friend Noodles, however, is always looking for trouble – and, somehow, it's always Ali who picks up the pieces. But, it's all small potatoes; it's not like anyone's getting hurt.

And then there's Needles. Needles is Noodles's brother. He's got a syndrome, and gets these ticks and blurts out the wildest things. It's cool, though: everyone on their street knows he doesn't mean anything by it.

But then Ali and Noodles and Needles find themselves somewhere they never expected to be . . . somewhere they never should've been – where the people aren't so friendly, and even less forgiving.